Oslo in April

John Slade

Oslo in April

ISBN 1-893617-11-4
Library of Congress Control Number:
2004092583

FIRST EDITION

FICTION

Thank you to
Sissel Kyrkjebø
for the song "Frøet"
on her album "Sissel"
Stageway Imp. Norge, 1986

WOODGATE INTERNATIONAL
P.O. Box 190
Woodgate, New York 13494
USA
www.woodgateintl.com

"Ja," said Johannes, "so Beethoven was responsible for strong coffee and strong pianos."

"Exactly," said Voldemar. "And something more. His belief was very strong. Which was important, because he believed in *us*. He lived in the age of Napoleon, an age of kings and tyrants and a tzar, and of unrelenting war. He earned his money from the fickle aristocracy. His publishers were, some of them, outright thieves. And yet he wrote music about Brotherhood, and Joy, and a God in Heaven. He wrote music for the ages, and he sent out his encouragement to every age. Because he believed in us."

КОНЦЕРТ № 5

Бетховен, Op. 73.

Adagio un poco mosso.

This novel is dedicated
to the first global generation
in human history.
Step forth.
With your university degrees,
your global communication,
and your commitment to
a better village,
a better country,
a better world,
step forth.
Bring your Singing Revolution.

Acknowledgements

From deep in my heart,
Thank you.

Anne Cecilie Kjelling
Ruth Johnson and Jon Simonsen
Ulf and Gro Lie
Lars Flæten
Peep Jahilo
Åge and Vigdis Lind
Einar Berglan
Edvard Rønning

Svetlana Mikhailovna Zhigulina

Audrey Sherman
Margaret Roberts
Marie Imundo
Ruth Fisher
Joe Antinarella
Elisa Pinzel
Cathy and Jeff Graver
Cheryl Shusdock
Al Brown

Utica Public Library, Utica, New York
National Public Radio

This novel is not a portrait of contemporary Norway.
It is first and foremost, a story.
No character in this novel is based on any actual person;
all characters are completely fictional.

But that first warm day in April,
when the golden sun shone down from a heaven of blue,
and the only snow left was in dirty heaps
along the roads and in the woods,
was very real.

Part I

A Cello Named Birkebeiner

CHAPTER 1

When he awoke from his first night alone in twenty-three years, he felt that the blood in his veins had been replaced by the blackest of ink. Because of mornings like this, he kept no gun in the house; otherwise he would have departed long ago. He had stayed alive for his daughters, though they had hardly noticed.

With enormous effort, he lifted his arm and laid it over his eyes, blocking out the faint glow of dawn through the bedroom window. He was vaguely aware—he could not think so enormous a thought—that he was supposed to conduct the orchestra tonight. A visiting pianist, a Beethoven concerto. Better that the orchestra played a brief funeral march, while he lay in absolute peace inside a coffin.

If he did not appear at the concert hall by seven-thirty, Bente would phone him, and get no answer. Someone would rush by car to his house and knock on the door.

He would by then have found a lake, deep in the forest north of the city, where the rotten ice of April would carry him until suddenly he broke through. The cold black water would caress him, take him home.

What did it matter? He had been dead now for almost twenty-one years. Her courtship (for surely *she* had courted him) had been a pretense, for once she had married him, she stopped coming to his concerts. She had her "practice," and was otherwise on call at the hospital. Her one enduring excuse did not mask the fact that as far as she was concerned, eighty percent of who he was did not exist.

He should have and should have and should have and should have left her. But they lost the first child, a boy, and bonded in their grief more deeply than in anything else. The next child, a girl, survived. As did their second daughter. He was by now so starved for love, that a toddling brat and a squalling infant promised to become

3

the bearers of some distant happiness. He had no other thought but to wait, and wait, and wait until the kids were old enough to become his friends. But a symphony is something difficult for two little girls to grasp, or enjoy.

And both of them certainly inherited their musical talent from their mother. Piano lessons lasted a dismal six months, gladly traded for skating lessons. The girls learned at an early age their mother's mocking laugh: Daddy was "waving his stick" tonight.

So he had lived two lives. One as the conductor of the Oslo Symphony Orchestra, working with musicians who shared with him a world both fragile and profound. And the other as a model father who should have roared, just once, with Beethoven's towering rage, at all that was squalid and petty and stagnant in his home.

Now the girls were off to their universities. And Thorunn, as if changing her shoes, had departed last night on the evening flight to be with her petroleum executive in Stavanger.

He was free. But the eighty percent had lived for so long without a breath of loving air, that only a husk now lay alone in bed. The blood running in his veins down to his wrists was as cold and black as the deep water which would welcome him. If he could somehow in the course of the day manage to drag himself out of bed, and out the door, and down the street to the trolley stop; and then to Sognsvann. He would walk along a trail through the forest until he found a lake where no one would be watching while he stared out at a sheet of gray rotten ice.

Anne Cecilie could play the A on her oboe tonight, and the orchestra could tune its strings and slides and timpani skin, quite well without him.

He was still lying on his back in bed, having done nothing more than lift one tired arm from his face and drop it onto the mattress, then lift his other arm and lay it over his eyes to block out the growing light of morning (he was vaguely aware that outside his open window, birds were twittering, and the stream was gurgling more noisily than usual with the springtime snow melt), when he heard four knocks on the front door downstairs, "Boom, boom, boom, BOOM," as if Beethoven were knocking.

Whoever it was—probably a kid selling lottery tickets for the school football team—he'd go away.

The problem was, it was the wrong season. It should be autumn, October, when the snow was just beginning to cover the ground. Not here in Oslo, but up north, in the mountains along the coast north of Bodø. He knew from his military service, twenty-five years ago, that an October storm blowing in from the sea would cover just the tallest peaks with white. When the storm ended, those peaks, towering in their ragged parade along the coastline, shone so brightly in the morning sun. If the day became especially clear, the October sun, low in the sky as it swung across the south, tinged the peaks with a warm soft pinkish-orange.

The next blizzard from the sea would blanket the mountain slopes with white. That's when he wanted to be there. Catch the day train from Oslo to Trondheim, the night train from Trondheim to Bodø. Take a taxi north out of town to the foot of the mountains, then with good boots and a rucksack filled with warm clothing, but no food, no tent, spend the day climbing the path he knew well until he found fresh snow on a northern slope. Find a bowl where the snow had not melted all summer. Then just lie down in that bowl at dusk, as comfortable as right here in this bed, and let the cold night do its work.

The next blizzard raging in from the sea would cover him with deep cold snow. How peaceful. How beautifully, beautifully peaceful. Six months later in April, when the snow began to melt, he would slowly sink, a dark mass in the shadow of the mountain. Or the wolves would find him, and just his bones would sink. Into deep cold snow in a bowl on the northern slope: snow that never melted.

"Johannes."

His body jolted with surprise. He lifted his arm and rolled his head on the pillow to look toward the bedroom door.

"Would you like a cup of coffee?"

It was Inger, his first violinist, the concertmaster, wearing a blue denim shirt and blue denim slacks, an outfit she might wear if she were working in the garden.

She held a steel thermos in one hand, a brown china cup in the other. He hadn't heard her open the door, hadn't heard her feet on the stairs. She had never been in his house before, and now she stood at the door to his bedroom. While he lay in bed like a bedraggled cadaver.

"Inger." His tired mind could think of nothing more.

"Johannes, we have the most beautiful April morning out there." Stepping into the room, she placed the brown cup on a night table where two photographs of his daughters had recently stood. Then she unscrewed a cup from the top of the thermos, set the steel cup beside the brown cup, and poured steaming dark coffee into both of them. "Sometimes, Johannes, we forget who we are. Because we haven't been ourselves for so long. During rehearsals this past week, we all wondered, 'Where is Johannes?' Your eyes didn't reach out to us. Your tempo was limp."

He smelled the coffee. It reminded him of making coffee in an old black pot over a campfire, in a forest where the sun shone warmly on thick pine needles on the ground. The smell of the brown needles—that reassuring summertime scent—mixed with the smell of the coffee were together like a perfectly matched flute and oboe playing a pastoral duet.

He stared at her hand holding the thermos as she poured: her right hand, which otherwise held and worked her bow. He looked at her left hand: at her strong fingers that usually scampered so deftly up and down the four strings. Now they wrapped around the brown mug as she offered it to him.

Embarrassed to be seen in such a state of weakness, he sat up in bed so that he could take the cup of coffee. He discovered that he was still wearing the rumpled maroon shirt and gray trousers which he had worn yesterday at rehearsal. He was like a drunk who had passed out in bed, except that he had not been drinking. "Thanks," he said as he took the warm cup, briefly touching Inger's fingers, not by choice, but by clumsiness.

"You're welcome."

She picked up the steel cup, then walked around the foot of the bed to the window. It was open a crack; he could hear the stream gurgling outside. She set her cup on the ledge, then she swung the window wide open: the sound of the stream seemed to leap into the room.

She peered out the window to the left, to the right, and up toward the sky while she drank her coffee. He could see from where he sat that the sky above the spruce was blue.

Then she turned to him and said, "My sailboat has been sleeping under a damp canvas all winter. I try to remember how happy I can be, when I'm out there on the fjord, racing with the wind. The sun sparkles on the waves. The gulls cry down, asking me if I have yet learned their language."

He drank the strong coffee, wanting it to go straight into his veins. "Inger, I'm not feeling very well. I think that Arne might take over tonight." Arne was the assistant conductor, a gifted student, awaiting his chance.

"Arne is preparing for his Grieg concert in May. You, tonight, Johannes Berg, will conduct, with deep understanding, the anguish and despair of Tchaikovsky's Sixth Symphony."

"I can't."

"I quite understand."

Inger was tall; he had always liked that she was almost as tall as he was. The light from the window backlit her long hair, more silver than blond. Slender in her blue slacks, standing with her customary dignity, she watched him, studied him. Of all the women in the world—and he had seen many in his travels as a pianist and conductor—he preferred the slender Scandinavian beauties of his native land.

Thus he had chosen Thorunn. But the nymph, so captivating when she flirted with him, proved to be without any comparable spirit. When she awakened in the morning beside him, she never heard, never imagined, the flute of Grieg's magical morning in the mountains; rather, she recited a grocery list, or reminded him of a car repair appointment. Hard to believe now that she was really gone. She should be calling him from the kitchen, "Your oatmeal's getting cold!"

"Johannes." Inger stood at the edge of the bed, on Thorunn's side. "If we are going to get where we need to go today, then I must speak quite freely."

As conductor and concertmaster, they had discussed countless times the pacing of a phrase, the fervor of a crescendo, the strength of an attack; then she would lead the strings while he reached out to the entire orchestra. As professionals working together over the years, they had never faltered. But as strangers without a score to follow, they had no experience at all.

He could see in her lovely brown eyes that she wanted to trust him. She had been brave enough to walk so unexpectedly into his life; now she needed the courage to invite him into hers.

"Johannes, I have been married to my violin all my life."

"I should have stayed married to my piano."

"Ja."

She sat on the foot of the bed, facing him. "I will not belabor you with poignant descriptions of long nights of aching loneliness. But I will tell you, Johannes, that I am now forty-two years old, and thus at the point, or beyond the point, when I may not be able to have a child." She did not look away as she revealed such a personal thought, but stared openly at him, allowing him to see the regret that would never leave her. "I was born a musician, and according to that merciless instinct, I have poured my love into music. I never knew, during those adolescent years of passionate determination, that there was any other price, any sacrifice, beyond the endless hours of practice. But now I know. And Johannes, sometimes the only way I can get myself out of bed in the morning," she nodded at him, meaning, I have been so often just like you, "is by telling myself that soon I will pour my enormous love into the music which I share with a hundred and seven members of one of the finest orchestras in the world."

She sipped her coffee, watching him, always watching him. He drank his own coffee, nearly emptied the cup.

Then she leaned forward and scolded him with her dark eyes. "But when I, when we, are gathered in rehearsal and our conductor does not bring out our best, does not *demand* our best, then the only thing that keeps me going in this world is no longer there. Johannes, for the past several years, little by little, I have watched you fading. During the past few months, you have been like a scarecrow with a baton. And this past week, when we discovered—I'm sorry, but it was so obvious—that you were spending the nights on a cot in your office, we began to wonder not why you were not reaching us, but how we could reach you."

"I'm sorry." Yes, I've got to make a phone call to Arne.

"I want you to understand, Johannes, that if you do not allow me to be whom I desperately need to be," she paused, "then I hear a child's voice, calling to me in the middle of the night."

"Inger, I should have talked with Arne long before the rehearsals began. He's quite capable of handling the Tchaikovsky, and the—"

"No. We are recording tonight, Johannes. The microphones are ready. We all know what you can do. Or used to do, four, five years ago. We all know what you can make us be. Or better put, what you can make us become. But we wonder where your spirit went. Where is our Johannes?"

He looked down at his feet under the white eiderdown, and thought of a bowl of snow on the northern slope of a mountain, where no one would expect anything of him, ever.

"I did not come here to blame you, Johannes. There is not a one of us who blames you. Pardon my saying so, but we have all been fully aware of the absence of Thorunn in the audience for the past decade or two. This is not normal, not right. Anne Cecilie's husband is a dairy farmer, out in the barn with his cows twice a day, but when she tunes us with her A before an evening concert, Odd is there in the front row, guaranteed."

She patted his feet under the eiderdown. "My boy, do you have any idea how much we hundred and eight musicians love you? We never say so, of course. We stand up to honor your entrance at the beginning of the program, and we let the audience provide the applause at the end. We put our violins and horns back into their cases and take the train home. We never tell you, or certainly never clearly enough, that you have built one of the finest orchestral voices in all of Europe. You have trained our once ramshackle brass until they have gained a most confident *svorzando*. You have turned Eli Margrethe from a student into a professional violinist in a mere eight months. Bjørn on the timpani has been invited—did you know this?—by London, but he turned them down, to be with you."

Her eyes filled with gratitude. "And what you have done for my strings, Johannes Berg, with your discipline and your determination and your once-upon-a-time fire, has enabled our violinists to reach the peak of their talent."

Then her eyes sharpened with anger. "So do you think that now we want to watch all that slip away, because, as we suppose, of some dreary wife? I am sorry, Johannes, if I have taken an unusual liberty this morning, but when word got around, as it will, that the Princess Who Was Too Good For You finally decided to re-establish her kingdom in Stavanger by the Sea, then it was time to wade into the wreckage to see if you were still alive. And you are, as I see," she smiled as she shook her head, "though it's going to take a bit more than a clean shirt to get you ready for tonight."

Was she really here, saying all this to him?

"Let me remind you that a young man from Estonia has been rehearsing with us all week. This is his first concert in the West, the first time he will be recorded in the West. And further, the concert will be broadcast live by radio to his people in Estonia. Voldemar has that concerto in him, there is no doubt about that. But he is baffled by the great Berg. Deeply disappointed. And wondering how he can give an extraordinary Beethoven's Fifth Piano Concerto to the world, as his proud gift from Estonia, when the conductor in rehearsal seems barely able to make it through the *Adagio*, much less give voice to the final triumph of the *Allegro*."

"Yes, I know I have failed him."

"No you have not. First Tchaikovsky. Then intermission. Then Rossini's galloping overture. And *then*, Johannes," she shook her finger at him with stern discipline, "you and Voldemar Keskküla will together be profound, magnificent, and triumphant."

It was so absurdly far beyond him. How much better if he had a fever. Or had broken a leg.

"Now," she stood up from the bed, "I shall see if the Princess has left any eggs in the kitchen, while you take a shower."

She was surprised at how happy she was, making breakfast for him, even in someone else's kitchen. She was especially pleased when she found a note on the counter, apparently the final message from Thorunn before the Old Witch departed:

> J,
> The cat seems to have disappeared at some point
> during the week.
>
>   T

Imagine calling him J, as if he no longer had a name, had been reduced to just a letter. He was Johannes of the Big Shoulders, able to raise and sweep his arms with his baton for hours at a time, in better shape probably than most tennis players.

She had carried a wicker basket into the kitchen with provisions for a breakfast: a cantaloupe, a block of cheese, and a loaf of bread (she had been out of eggs). In the trunk of the car was a box of food, especially potatoes. Breakfast for two; then lunch for three, she hoped, out on the boat. She would try to catch a codfish for dinner. Then they would sail up the fjord to the Oslo wharf, and walk up the hill together to the Concert House. She had her black dress in the car. She'd make sure he brought his suit, socks, shoes, everything he needed for the concert tonight. Once she got him out the door, there'd be no coming back to where he had been so miserable.

She had a cheese and mushroom omelette well under way, and was scolding the Witch for the most paltry assortment of spices in the cupboard—didn't the woman ever make her man a real meal?—when Johannes appeared in the kitchen doorway, looking a bit better: he was freshly shaven, and wearing an old brown shirt and trousers that he no doubt wore when puttering around the house on a Saturday. But the exhaustion was still in his eyes, as if he had just barely managed to crawl out of a sick bed.

She asked him, "Shall we eat out on the porch in the sunshine?" She had noticed, during a quick glance around the house while he was in the shower, a porch off the living room, overlooking the yard. The morning sun shone fully upon it, although the wooden chairs and round table were covered with wet brown leaves from last autumn.

"By the time you brush off the chairs, I'll have everything ready. Would you like me to make another pot of coffee?"

"Inger." She could see tears running down his cheeks. Yes, the tears had to come out, before anything else could begin.

And then he told her (as he often told some small story to the orchestra, about the composer whose music they were playing), "Beethoven admired very few people at the keyboard, especially when they played his own works. But one musician whom he greatly admired was a woman—something rare in those days of male musicians—a woman named Dorothea, Baroness von Ertmann, whom all of Vienna knew as one of his finest interpreters." Johannes raised a hand and brushed his wet cheek.

"When Dorothea lost her first child, shortly after its birth, she was unable to weep at the funeral. She grieved in silence for several days in her house, and received no visitors. Finally her husband, General Ertmann, took her to visit their friend Beethoven. Beethoven had of course learned of her loss, and invited them into his somewhat untidy apartment. As he sat down at his piano, he said to Dorothea, 'We will now converse in music.' He played for her until she began to sob, and he kept playing, reaching from his own heart deeper and deeper into hers, until finally her grief had poured out and she found some comfort."

Inger lifted the half-cooked omelette from the burner and set it on a cold corner of the stove, then she turned off the burner. "Do you have the *Adagio* that Voldemar will play tonight?"

Johannes nodded, then disappeared from the doorway into the living room.

Grateful that he trusted her, grateful that he was willing to do what needed to be done, she wiped her hands with a dish towel, then joined him in the living room.

He was putting a record on a turntable. He handed her the record cover, then he sat on the edge of a sofa and leaned forward with his face in his hands.

She looked at the cover, saw that of course it was a classic: Sir Georg Solti conducting the Chicago Symphony Orchestra, with Vladimir Ashkenazy on piano. Both men were pictured, deep in their work of conducting and playing, against a black background. She turned the cover over and read: 1973. Tonight, thirty years later, Johannes and Voldemar would seek to reach such heights.

She looked at the record, already spinning on the turntable, to be sure that it was on side two, then she cued the needle down to the beginning of the *Adagio*, the second movement of the three-part concerto. While sound crackled from two tall speakers, she sat beside Johannes on the sofa. Her bow was poised, waiting for the first sweep of his baton.

The muted violins, over a *pizzicato* bass, began their slow gentle melody. Every few bars, the sound was enriched: by the bass now no longer plucked but played with a bow; by the entrance of the flute, clarinet, and bassoon, blending almost imperceptibly with the strings; by the entrance of the viola, deepening the strings. And yet there were pauses, quarter-note rests, moments of silence, as if the orchestra were stepping quietly toward someone sleeping, someone very beautiful, someone about to wake up.

The piano awoke with the lightest possible touch on a pair of notes an octave apart: a grace note hopping up to a clear sustained F sharp. She sometimes imagined, while her strings played *pianissimo* through those first sixteen bars, that a mother was stepping quietly toward her infant in a cradle, and then the child blinked open his eyes.

The piano did not leap to life, but stirred with a gradually increasing vitality, quietly singing, *pianissimo cantabile.* She heard the first trill, admired Ashkenazy's smooth, astonishingly rapid touch; the child's eyes not only perceived the world, but gave off a brief spark of life. A tiny laugh. The first faint glimpse of confidence.

As the piano gained a tentative strength, rising and falling with clear rapid pairs of notes, and then played solo for two bars while the entire orchestra rested, she knew that Johannes was inside the music. He leaned forward, his strong back arching beside her. His elbows were on his knees, his hands were pressed against his face.

He had left the shabby world of recrimination and failure, and had entered a delicate world of gentle beauty. A world of peace, peace which the heart could grasp within an unhurried flow of time.

It was during a passage of trills, moving up half-step by half-step through fifteen notes, buoyed by the gentlest of *crescendos,* that his whole body clenched, and then the sobs burst out. Without a moment's thought she reached her hands to his powerful shaking shoulders and held the strongest man she had ever held while he wailed like a lost broken child. She laid her cheek on the curve of his convulsing back and heard both the music drawing his grief out of him, and the grief itself, like orchestra and piano: a concerto of despair.

The *Adagio,* eight and a half minutes long, now quieted as it approached the attack on the *Rondo* of the third movement. She released her grip on his shoulders, stood up from the sofa and stepped to the record player, ready to lift the needle. The tempo of the music slowed, then the orchestra rested while the piano nearly fell back asleep, sustaining at the very end of the movement a solitary B-natural . . .

She cued up the needle. The room was silent. After a long moment, he lifted his face from his hands and managed, through the devastation in his eyes, a faint smile. "Ja," he said, "even better than coffee."

"Johannes, once more, all right?"

He nodded.

"This time, think of the boy from Estonia who wants to play this *Adagio* tonight. He is twenty-three, a couple of years older than your daughters."

Johannes stared at her. Was she asking too much of him, too

soon?

He sat up straight on the edge of the sofa, his hands on his knees. "Ja."

She lowered the needle, then she sat beside him on the edge of the sofa. The muted strings began their slow song. The plucked bass strings, with a rest between each deep pair of notes, counted slow, distinct seconds on a clock that did not measure time, did not rush time, but graciously and generously provided all the time in the world.

She could not know what he thought about adopting a son tonight, if only for one three-movement concerto, lasting forty minutes. After all, what did she know about parents and children? But at least, as with Dorothea, Baroness von Ertmann, that first hideous anguish no longer clenched his heart in its grip. For the sobs had ended; he listened to the music now as if in a trance.

As the *Adagio* stepped on gossamer tones toward the final sustained B, he stood up from the sofa, crossed the room and lifted the needle. He set the needle in its cradle, lowered the plastic lid over the turntable, switched off the power.

"Ja," he said, turning toward her. "I thank you, Inger, for a most beneficial rehearsal."

"You are most welcome," she said, standing up from the sofa. "Now if you will brush the leaves off the chairs on the porch, I will see about our omelette."

They sat outside in the early morning sunshine, savoring what promised to be a magnificent springtime day. She watched him eat two-thirds of the omelette, two large slices of perfectly ripe melon, and three slices of bread—with herring, then liver paste, then strawberry jam—as if the poor man had been starved for a month. He didn't want her to make another pot of coffee, but drank nearly a full liter of orange juice. He thanked her as he settled back in his chair, then he lifted his face, closed his eyes, and simplified his existence to the sacred and eternal Scandinavian ritual of basking, after the unrelenting ordeal of winter, in the life-giving balm of the sun.

She looked up at the crystalline blue sky, without a cloud anywhere, while she listened to the happy gurgling of a stream that coursed along the lower edge of the yard. A breeze stirred the boughs of a row of spruce along the opposite bank, reminding her that out on the fjord, a steady wind from the south was waiting to fill her sails. She felt the old restlessness that her mother and father had always felt: to be out on the water.

"This morning," said Johannes, his face still lifted like a mask of serenity toward the sun, "when I first woke up, I wanted to go back to sleep for a thousand years. Now, just a hundred would do."

A cluster of starlings swooped down and landed in a bare birch tree, the first starlings that she had seen this spring. She listened to their raspy chatter as they shifted restlessly from branch to branch. Reddish buds, though not yet leaves, were visible on the tips of the birch twigs.

"Johannes, don't forget that you have an appointment at ten o'clock."

Opening his eyes, he stared at her, baffled. "An appointment?"

"Well, nothing formal. But I do think you should phone Voldemar, so that the two of you can go through the score together. Otherwise the poor boy is left with nothing more than the, shall we say, inadequate preparation under the conductor's baton during the past week. I think you owe it to him, Johannes. Don't make him worry all day about some impending disaster tonight."

Johannes closed his eyes and leaned back in his chair with a weary sigh. "Inger, how am I possibly going to do this?"

She knew of only one kind of magic, though she could not promise whether it would prove powerful enough. "I don't think that you should work together in the concert hall. It's too nice a day. Voldemar is not staying at the hotel," which, she did not say, was no place to leave alone a completely distraught young foreigner, "but with Per Olaf at his farm. I think we should drive to Ås, pick up Voldemar, then drive down to the harbor at Drøbak. We'll take the tarp off the boat, pull the sails out of their bags, open our beautiful white wings and let the wind do all the work. We can anchor at lunchtime, and while you two are busy with your *allegros*, I'll try to catch us a codfish. What do you say?"

Johannes looked at her, too tired to say yes, too tired to say no.

"Johannes, bring your maestro's tails aboard, and I'll bring my dress. Voldemar can bring whatever sort of suit they wear in Estonia. We shall dock at the Aker Wharf at seven o'clock, stroll up the hill together to the Concert House, and greet the orchestra with a bit of sunshine on our cheeks."

He leaned forward in his chair and peered down from the porch into the yard. Following his gaze, she saw a row of five white boxes perched along a stone wall. Now she spotted the bees, glittering in the sunshine as they streamed in and out of each box.

"They're just waking up," he said. "No flowers yet, but they want to stretch their wings."

She waited. It was his decision. She could only offer; she could not force him.

Watching the bees, he said, "We'd have to stop at my office to pick up the score."

"Voldemar will certainly have his own score. It might be helpful if you looked through his notes, rather than he at yours."

A gust of wind blew through the spruce along the far side of the stream. She and Johannes watched the thick green boughs lifting and bobbing, until the *crescendo* of wind faded.

"Beethoven," said Johannes, "wrote his Fifth Piano Concerto while Napoleon was besieging Vienna with artillery. If Beethoven could hear the *Adagio* with cannons in the background, then who am I to complain about a small domestic disaster?"

She took the two plates into the kitchen and rinsed them while the Maestro phoned Per Olaf, then asked to speak with Voldemar. She heard Johannes's voice, now speaking in English, come to an abrupt halt. After half a minute of silence, she glanced from the kitchen door into the living room and saw Johannes with a hand over his bowed face as he listened to the phone. All the progress she had made seemed ready to collapse.

Finally he said, "Voldemar, I fully understand. You do not come alone. You represent your people. I'm sorry, Voldemar. You see, I've been through a very difficult month or two."

Again he was silent, listening. He lowered his hand from his face, looked for a chair, sank into it. "Yes, I understand. Your people have been through a very difficult eight hundred years."

Inger touched his shoulder, then she took the phone and spoke in English, "Voldemar, this is Inger Magnussen, the concertmaster. I suggest that you and Johannes Berg spend the afternoon going over the score together, until you are both satisfied that you are ready for the concert tonight. Yes, yes, please listen to me. I suggest that we pick you up in an hour, then the three of us will drive to a nearby harbor on the fjord, where I have my sailboat. I think we first need some fresh air and sunshine, and then we can settle down to business. You will have quite the opportunity to discuss every measure of all three movements, I assure you. What do you say? Can I count on you as crew? You don't get seasick, do you?"

She listened to him tell her, in a much calmer voice, that in fact his girlfriend's family had a sailboat, moored in Tallinn's harbor. She looked at Johannes and nodded that everything would be all right.

"Fine, then. Voldemar," she looked at her watch, "it's five to nine now. We shall be at Per Olaf's house by ten-fifteen, ten-thirty at the latest. Please wear something warm for the boat. Per Olaf will help you with a sweater, and perhaps a pair of sneakers. Bring your suit for tonight, and your score, for we shall not be returning to the farm. We'll be going directly from the sailboat to the Concert House."

All he needed, Voldemar said, was an hour with the conductor, two at the most. It was the tempos that especially needed fixing. She heard the optimism in his voice, the eagerness that everything truly would be all right.

"Yes, you will have exactly every tempo that you need, Voldemar. I promise you that. See you soon. Bye-bye."

She set the phone in its cradle, and felt enormously tired. She was going to be Captain today, on a most difficult voyage. "Johannes, just let him say all that he wants to tell you. Once he has gotten it out, I think you will find that he's a brilliant pianist, ready to give you a superb performance."

Johannes stood up from the chair and nodded. He was ready to at least give it a try.

She touched her fingertips to his freshly shaven cheek. "All you need to do, Johannes, is be our Maestro . . . the Maestro whom we know you can be."

"Ja," he said. "We go sailing."

CHAPTER 2

Astrid awoke with an immediate sense of joyous anticipation, for today was her seventieth birthday. She would play the cello for her mother in the morning, then she would play for her father in the early afternoon. Magnus would take her picture, a birthday portrait. Then she and her family of fifteen (along with seven of her students and whatever mothers and fathers wanted to come along), would take the train south from Lillehammer to Oslo, where her twelve other students, all of them refugees or the children of refugees, would meet her (again with whatever mothers and fathers wanted to come along), at the Oslo train station. Then all together (Magnus would carry her cello), they would walk as a grand parade along Karl Johan Boulevard, past old sour Ibsen at the National Theater, to the grand, glass-enclosed, splendidly lit entrance to the Concert House. Where she would play tonight the cello solo that opened Rossini's overture.

From the age of ten to the age of seventy with her cello: yes, not so bad a job in that. Only Magnus, who had first kissed her at the age of eight, could surpass those sixty years.

She rolled her head on the pillow to look at Magnus: he was awake of course. And smiling at her, of course. It wasn't that he awoke before she did, but that he always sensed when she awoke, and so he did too.

"Congratulations on your day," he said to her, then he rolled up on one shoulder, reached his face toward her and kissed her on the lips.

He lay back on his pillow and narrowed his eyes at the ceiling while he pondered. "Now let me see. If today you are seventy, and we have been married for fifty-one years, then . . ." He frowned at the difficulty of the calculation. "Ja, we were eight when I fell in love with you, so therefore . . ." He grumbled while he cogitated, then suddenly he sat up in his blue pajamas and grinned down at her with genuine delight, "I have loved you for sixty-two years!"

"Ever since your first cup of spring water."

"Jaah." He still said 'jaah' like an old mountain farmer. She loved him for that. He tossed away the eiderdown on his side of the bed and stood up. "I shall be back in five minutes with your coffee." His white hair was tussled, his pajamas were rumpled, but he gave her a slight formal bow. Taking his brown bathrobe from its bedpost, he slid his feet into his slippers—their slippers had been side by side for fifty-one years—and hurried into the kitchen.

Snuggling deeper under the warm eiderdown, she remembered his first birch cup of spring water. She and her father had been visiting a neighboring farmer, and while the men discussed some business, Magnus, whom she knew from school, invited her to see a new calf in the upper pasture. The day was warm, in early June, and as they climbed the hill, Magnus asked her if she would like a drink "of water almost as cold as ice." She said yes, so he led her on a path to a grove of birch, their fluttering leaves still springtime green. In the middle of the grove was a cluster of mossy boulders; between two of them, water gurgled out of the ground and formed a tiny creek. Atop one of the boulders was a cup carved from a birch burl. Magnus dipped the cup into the spring, then he handed it to her; it had a carved handle with one hole for her finger.

The water was so cold that it hurt her teeth. "You're right," she told him, "It's almost ice."

He watched her as she emptied the cup. She handed it back to him.

He grinned. "More?"

Wanting to please him, she said, "Yes."

He dipped the cup into the gurgling spring, handed it to her, and again watched her as she drank water from deep in the cold heart of the mountain. It was like the water from her own well, but in January.

Then Magnus took the cup and drank from the spring, first one brimming cup, and then, as if to do the same as she had done, a second cup. He set the empty cup atop the boulder, then he stared at her with a look of wonder. He leaned forward, kissed her quickly on the cheek, then he bolted out of the shady grove into the sunshine, calling back to her not in triumph but with jubilant devotion, "I love you! I love you! I love you!"

He stopped on the path and turned around, waiting for her; waiting, perhaps, to see if she was angry.

She was not angry. She did not hold his hand as they walked along the path and up the trail the rest of the way to see the calf. But neither did she scold him. He did not kiss her again until they both were sixteen.

But there was never a day, not even during the war, that could possibly have been complete without their speaking to each other, or at least writing a note to each other, to be delivered secretly from hand to hand after church on Sunday. And never once was he jealous of her cello.

Her father gave her the cello when she was ten. Or rather, he passed it on to her, had it delivered to her, as a temporary gift from someone to whom it really belonged. And to whom it still belonged, she believed, even sixty years later. She would be so grateful if the original owner suddenly appeared.

But until then, she would do as her father had done during the war: in her own way, she would lead people on a difficult path over the mountains, to safety, to freedom. To a new life.

Her father had not been fond of guns. Though many of the other farmers in the valley took up arms against the Germans early in the war, and later resorted to sabotage, that was not Papa's way. Rather, he was increasingly sought after as a guide on secret journeys over the mountains to Sweden. Sometimes it was a man in the Resistance who had been identified by the Germans, and thus needed to disappear.

A knock on the door in the night aroused her father, who had his rucksack and skis ready. Who had a dozen pairs of skis ready in the barn, and a dozen rucksacks.

Once the fellow was English; she had sat up in bed, listening to the strange language, and she was proud that her father could speak a few words in return.

Often her father was called to go elsewhere in Norway. Although he did not know the mountains north or south of Lillehammer as well as he knew the peaks and ranges and lakes and passes between his own home and Sweden, he could cross any wild country, summer or winter, and get his people over the border. When he came home, he never told his children where he had been or whom he had guided. After the war, however, he did say once, "I never lost a one. Not a man, woman, or child."

When she was almost ten—it was early in April of 1943 and her birthday was coming on the fifth—Papa was gone. A wagon rolled up to the farmhouse and the driver asked first for Kristine Marie Bjørnson—that was Mama—and then for Astrid Marie Bjørnson. That a stranger should appear in the yard and ask for her by name was truly extraordinary. She stood shyly beside her mother in the doorway while Mama spoke to the man. Satisfied that he had found the right place, the driver climbed down from the wagon seat, lifted a tarp from the back of the wagon, then hefted up from a bed of straw a black leather case that looked as if it might contain a giant fiddle. "Miss Astrid, here is your cello."

The man brushed off the leather case with a rag, then he carried it into the house and laid it on the kitchen table. She and her brothers clustered around him as he unfastened two latches and lifted the lid. Inside was what looked like, yes, a giant fiddle. But it was, as the man said, a cello. Made of reddish wood, with four strings.

"Your father sent it from Oslo. And there's some music too."

The man—he had a beard about half-grown, as if he were well on the way to hiding his face—went back out to the wagon, then returned with an expensive-looking suitcase.

He set it on the bench beside the table, unlocked two latches with a key, then lifted the lid. The suitcase was filled with what we recognized—but certainly could not read—as sheets of music.

By the time Papa returned home, two or three weeks later, Astrid had done nothing more than take the cello out of its case, once, and pluck its four strings. However, Lillehammer had a long tradition of attracting painters and writers and musicians, and thus Papa had little trouble in finding her a teacher. She began to make the trips into town once a week with her cello; her brother Ole drove her in the farm wagon, then he visited shops while she had her lesson. She quickly fell in love with the big unwieldy instrument that had a voice hidden inside it.

Magnus was never jealous. He never made fun of a farm girl playing such an elegant instrument. He never tried to pull her away from the hours that she spent practicing. And he never missed a concert, as the surprisingly talented girl quickly advanced beyond the other children in town and, at the age of fourteen, joined an ensemble of adults.

When the war was over and the Germans had departed and people could talk again without being afraid, Papa told her that he had helped an entire family, a Jewish family, to escape from Oslo to Sweden. One of the daughters, "a young woman of maybe twenty," had to leave her cello behind. While she and her family were packing what they would take from the apartment in the middle of the night, the woman asked Papa if *he* had a daughter. He said yes, then accepted the gift because he hated to think of the cello lost to the Nazis. He arranged for a driver and wagon. The cello was the only gift, during all five years of the war, that Papa ever brought or shipped home.

He never learned the woman's name, nor even the family's name. There were eight of them, including a child of five. He guided them, in late March and early April when the snow was still good and the sun shone longer and longer into the evening, through the deep silent forests to Sweden.

Astrid had waited during the first year after the war, and during the second year, for a young woman to appear at the farmhouse door, asking for her cello. Or at least, a letter should have arrived, addressed to her father, from a family in Sweden, or perhaps Oslo again, asking for the cello. But no one ever came, and no letter arrived. The people probably never knew Papa's name, and certainly not his address.

But that did not matter. The cello never belonged to Astrid; it was a temporary gift, even now, sixty years later. If, after the concert tonight, a woman her mother's age appeared backstage and told her that in April of 1943, she had fled to Sweden and left her cello behind, Astrid would gladly—ja, with deep, deep gratitude—return the precious gift.

Until then, her job was to guide, with the cello that she had named *Birkebeiner,* as many people as she could across their own difficult mountains, to safety, to freedom, to a new life.

Magnus appeared at the bedroom door, his blue eyes catching the light of the low morning sun through the window. His white hair was neatly brushed. He wore a green apron over his brown bathrobe. "Your coffee is ready, my love. But shall we have it out on the porch? Spring has finally arrived."

"Ja." She tossed away the eiderdown, swung her feet out of bed, took her lavender robe from the second bedpost, slid her feet into her slippers, then she followed him down the hallway and through the kitchen—which smelled of oatmeal and eggs and toast and coffee—to the door out to the back porch. On the old picnic table, between his bowl of oatmeal and hers, stood a vase with a dozen roses, jubilantly red in the morning sunshine.

"Magnus!"

He lifted his arms in readiness. "May I have this dance?"

She should have stopped to wash her face, to brush her hair, even to brush her teeth, but he did not mind. He had swept the porch completely, and so had transformed it, for the first time since last summer, into their dance hall. He took her hand, wrapped his other hand lightly around her waist, then he hummed a waltz from Tchaikovsky's "Sleeping Beauty" as they turned in each other's arms beneath a sky as blue as her husband's jubilant blue eyes.

And so they began, on the bedrock of their love, to build another day.

CHAPTER 3

Per Olaf, barely awake, slid one foot beneath the blanket, but felt no heavy lump where Murphy should have been. He slid his other foot in the other direction: no Murphy. The dog was always the last one out of bed. Actually, it was the absence of the lump that had awakened Per Olaf in the first place. Something was wrong.

Murphy was half English sheep dog and half Norwegian potato. He could herd the cows, the goats, the chickens, or whatever else needed to be brought in from the pasture to the barn. And he could dig. He never dug in the garden, he was good about that. But anywhere else in the pasture, in the orchard, in the woods, he could dig and dig and dig until the fluffy gray-white dog became increasingly brown-black, and the bowl of claw-scratched earth was big enough that Murphy could roll in it, rubbing his back and the top of his head into the damp soil until some ancient instinct was satisfied by the transformation from civilized dog to prehistoric earth monster. Then he would trot with utter content back to the porch and curl up in the sunshine, his feet drawn up and his nose tucked into his belly, looking very much like a giant, freshly dug potato.

If anyone on the farm had the time and inclination (it was usually Per Olaf), Murphy got a bath. Only after a bath, as Murphy well knew, was he allowed to sleep on the bed. And that privilege lasted only as long, as Murphy well knew, until he went digging again. It was the great moral dilemma in the dog's life: whether to luxuriate all night upon the big bed (on his own flannel blanket) between Per Olaf's feet and Ingeborg's feet, unwilling to budge an inch despite their sleepy prodding, or whether to dig down through the rich black soil to the cool damp sand beneath it, immersing himself and then covering himself, and nearly embalming himself, in the pungent, irresistible smells of the earth.

With a groan, Per Olaf rolled from his stomach onto his back, then lifted his head and peered in the faintly lit room at the foot of the bed: no Murphy. Just a rumpled empty flannel blanket. Ingeborg, on her side with her back toward him, was sound asleep. He peered out the window, wide open and without a screen—he had taken down all the screens to wash them—and saw the first faint glow of dawn. On a Saturday morning, he was certainly entitled to go back to sleep for another hour. A couple of cows were lowing, ready to be milked, but Odd and Anne Cecilie would soon be out in the barn to tend to them.

Then he spotted Murphy, a pale blur bounding across the dark farmyard. How did the darn dog get outside?

Per Olaf remembered the young man from Estonia, the guest pianist, all knotted up in a silent rage. Following that first disastrous rehearsal on Wednesday, Voldemar had been his house guest for the past three nights. Per Olaf was, in addition to being principal trumpeter, the chairman of the Foreign Guests Committee, a job which usually provided him with the great pleasure of meeting musicians from around the world. In this case, however, given Johannes's state of collapse, the job entailed much more than serving as the conscientious liaison: making sure that the hotel was all right, that the guest had adequate boots and mittens. In this case, Per Olaf had to make sure that the temperamental guest did not disappear to the airport and fly back home to Tallinn. So he had invited Voldemar Keskküla to stay at the farmhouse on Wednesday, Thursday and Friday night, with the hope that somehow he could calm the young man, and keep him in Norway until the concert on Saturday evening.

Voldemar must have gotten up during the night; then Murphy, hearing a stranger stirring in the house, had hopped out of bed. Voldemar must be outside; Murphy had gone out the door with him. The Estonian pianist might be walking at this very moment with his suitcase toward the highway, ready to thumb a ride at dawn to the nearest train station, and thence to the airport.

Careful not to wake Ingeborg, Per Olaf sat up on the edge of the bed. He groaned a second time. He did not like psychological problems. He was fundamentally a farmer, had grown up on this farm and still loved to spend an entire day on the tractor, turning the earth. His sister and her husband took care of the cows; he had grown tired long ago of the imprisonment of milking twice a day.

But he loved to plow, whether in preparation for turnips or potatoes. He loved to till Ingeborg's garden in the spring, stepping again and again on the blade of a shovel as he prepared a bed of black soil for her. As soon as the snow melted, he loved to walk over the rolling brown hills, where Norwegians had farmed for the past five thousand years. Although he and his sister had both been born musicians, taking their talent from their mother's side, and although he thus had to contend with temperamental artists far more than he would have liked—including at present a conductor who should have been shipped off to the Canary Islands for a month—he much preferred the simplicity and dependability and quiet beauty of rolling farmland.

So to have a brooding stranger in his house—even though the stranger had been invited by the Oslo Symphony Orchestra, and even though the cause of the brooding was perfectly clear and understandable—was very difficult for Per Olaf to contend with. He felt like a farmer aboard an open fishing boat in a storm at sea, called upon to man an oar while he and the rest of the crew struggled through heaving waves toward a safe harbor. He had little experience with an oar, and had no idea where that safe harbor might be.

Standing up from the bed—both knees creaked—he took off his pajamas and laid them neatly beside Murphy's empty blanket. He stepped into his jeans, pulled a sweater over his head, then sat on a chair and pulled on yesterday's wool socks. Stopping at the bathroom, he peed and washed his face. To make himself presentable for his guest (unless his guest had completely disappeared), he brushed his hair and brushed his teeth. He walked through the dark kitchen, slid his feet into rubber boots, then stepped out the door into the farmyard and automatically looked up. Only the brightest stars were still visible in the pale turquoise sky: his eyes jumped from cluster to cluster of summer stars. They were high overhead now on an April's dawn, as they would later be at midnight in August.

He scanned the horizon of rolling dark hills, from the purple-black western sky to the pearlescent east: not a cloud. The air was warm, the drift of wind—he lifted his face—from the south. The day promised to be the first triumphant day of spring, when unveiled sunshine would begin to warm the earth. He wanted to go back into the house to fetch his trumpet. He would walk with his horn (and with Murphy, of course) south along the ridge while the dawn brightened. Then, when the sun itself peeked over the hills to the southeast, he would turn and look back at the first touch of sunlight on the tall red barn. On the upper windows of the two white houses that flanked the barn. And on the round leafless crowns of the chestnut trees in the yard.

While the birds twittered in the spruce woods, and the farm itself stirred to life, he would play a fanfare. The strong, quick, bright, brassy notes would sail out over the countryside, announcing not the arrival of some king, but of life itself to the dormant land. Per Olaf was the leading fanfare trumpeter in Europe; he had recently cut a CD in London of historic British fanfares. Today, he would gladly have announced not Henry the Eighth, but the first gorgeous day of Spring.

However, Murphy now trotted across the yard toward a dark figure leaning against the garden fence. It was Voldemar, who, thank God, had not disappeared. Per Olaf knew that he would have to talk, or try to talk, with the young man. No trumpet this morning; he had to take care of a major psychological problem, or there would be no trumpet tonight.

Voldemar ignored the dog that nuzzled him with its nose, expecting a scratch on the head and maybe a walk together. But when he heard approaching footsteps, he turned his face toward Per Olaf. He was fully dressed: white shirt and tie, suitcoat, long black overcoat. His gloved hands gripped the top rail of the fence. Though a young man of twenty-three, with bushy dark hair and a slender frame, he carried himself with the authority of someone much older. Not only was his talent unusually well developed; so was his understanding of the world, and his own place in it.

"Good morning," said Per Olaf in English. "You are up early."

"I refuse," said Voldemar, the anger in his voice barely controlled, "to stand in the shadow of a dead tree."

"Ja." Per Olaf stood next to Voldemar at the fence, put his hands on the rough wooden rail and stared down at the unraked garden, littered with sticks and brown leaves from the winter. Murphy bumped his leg, expecting a walk. "I phoned Inger Magnussen last night, after you went to bed. She is our principal violinist. She will speak with Johannes Berg this morning, to make sure that the two of you can go over the score together."

"As I was promised we would do," Voldemar retorted, "when the conductor and I spoke in February on the phone. But all this week, there was no conductor on the podium. Only a ghost. And yesterday, at the end of rehearsal, the ghost simply vanished. Not a word about time for the two of us to go through the score. Does he think that the staggering death march which he conducted yesterday is what Beethoven had in mind for the final *Allegro?* That was the most lifeless tempo I have ever been forced to play. And then the conductor vanishes! Does the man even know that I sit there at the piano?"

"Ja." Per Olaf wondered if Inger would make any progress today with Johannes. Quite possibly she could, because no one had yet tried. Hard for a mere musician to tell the Maestro that he has become a catastrophe.

Voldemar stated once more, so to be absolutely understood, "Mr. Eide, I will not stand in the shadow of a dead tree."

Per Olaf nodded. "Voldemar, we are all as concerned as you are with the present condition of our conductor. Maestro Berg has been struggling with . . . with the collapse of his marriage, to be entirely truthful." He paused, then he added with a tone of hope, "But I do believe that Maestro Berg will pull himself quite together by this evening."

"Pull himself together?" Voldemar glared at him, his contempt unhidden. "Somehow I expected something more of the West."

Per Olaf watched a crow flapping in the distance across the milky blue sky. Looking up, he saw that most of the summer stars had vanished. "Voldemar—"

"I did not come here for myself alone. I come here as a voice from Estonia. A voice to tell Norway, to tell Europe, to tell the world, that we exist. The concert tonight will be broadcast live in Estonia. Did you know that? My people will be listening, not just to hear if their son can play well. Not just to hear beautiful, powerful music. They will be listening to hear what I will say, on their behalf, to the rest of the world. They want to hear me tell the world that Estonia is alive and flourishing." Voldemar added harshly, "They do not want to hear that once again we have been forgotten, ignored. As we have been for most of a century."

Per Olaf nodded. "Ja, that was part of our initial reasoning when we invited you to join us for this concert in April. We wanted, well, we thought, why invite someone from Berlin, or London, or New York, when we could perhaps enable someone from a smaller country to make his way in the world." Per Olaf did not like the reasonings and subtleties behind things; he much preferred a jubilant brassy fanfare to announce the arrival of something wonderful.

"And for that I thank you." Voldemar's voice softened. "For that, Estonia says thank you to Norway."

The two men stood shoulder to shoulder, their hands on the rail, staring beyond the garden toward the distant rolling contours of cleared and wooded land. A brief truce had been established between them.

Very brief. "Do you know," said Voldemar, "that there are fewer Estonians living in Estonia today than there were in 1939? First Stalin, then Hitler, and then Stalin again. For us, World War Two did not end until 1991."

Voldemar thumped his gloved fist on the fence railing. "For eight hundred years, we have been beneath somebody's boot. The Danes, the Prussians, the Russians, the Germans, the Russians again. Countless thousands of my people are buried in Siberia." He pointed at the long dark green edge of the spruce forest. "Estonia had twenty years of freedom between the two world wars. For twenty years, we came out from the forests where we had been hiding for centuries, into the sunshine of freedom. Then in 1940, Stalin's troops marched in, and we had to hide in the forest again. For a brutal half century. Until we broke free in 1991. Mr. Eide, during the past eight hundred years, since the time when the rest of Europe was building its first cathedrals, we have been somebody's vassal. Somebody's slave. Somebody's prisoner. In almost a millennium, we had only twenty years of independence. And now, since 1991, another twelve." Voldemar's dark eyes burned with intense determination. "And I am here to say, on behalf of my people, who stood in Stalin's shadow, who stood in the Soviet shadow, that never again will we stand in the shadow of a dead man. Or a dead government. Or a dead idea."

"Ja, now I begin to understand."

"This is not just a piano concerto. I am playing tonight for the thousands of people buried in the frozen tundra of Siberia. I am playing for the thousands who are buried in the Estonian earth. And

I am playing tonight for our children, who are learning to type English into their computers. I am playing tonight to say, 'We wish to become citizens of the world.'"

"Ja, so we wanted too under Denmark, under Sweden."

Voldemar smiled, the first smile that Per Olaf had seen all week. "I can thank you for one thing," he said. "Norway never conquered us."

Per Olaf laughed in agreement. "Nei, all our Vikings sailed off to Ireland and Iceland. The ones who stayed home were nice quiet farmers and fishermen. We have always preferred our own rocks to somebody else's soil."

"Yes, farmers," said Voldemar with a tone almost of reverence. "We call ourselves *Maarahvas*, the people of the land." He swept his gloved hand toward the pasture and distant potato fields. "I look at your farm, and I am almost home."

They heard someone approaching behind them. Turning, they saw Anne Cecilie, Per Olaf's sister, the orchestra's oboist, walking toward them from the second farmhouse with a cup of coffee in each hand.

"Good morning, gentlemen. Unless the chickens are on strike, I shall have an omelette ready in about half an hour." She offered them each a cup of steaming coffee.

"Takk."

"Thank you very much."

She looked at Voldemar with that instinctive compassion which Per Olaf had known in his sister since they were children. Whether it was a troubled playmate or an injured sparrow, she knew who was hurt, and did something to fix it. "We all know how you feel, Voldemar. I apologize on behalf of the orchestra that we did not say more to you about the situation. We are too professional, minding our jobs, hoping that somehow all will go well. We are a quiet people, sometimes too quiet." Voldemar nodded, waiting for more.

Anne Cecilie continued, "You have seen our conductor at his absolute worst. Even we have never experienced Johannes Berg as he has been this past week. But we have also seen him conducting from the mountaintop. Bringing us, *all* of us, right up there with him."

Voldemar drank his coffee; above the cup, his dark intense eyes were skeptical.

Already in her work clothes before the sun was up, Anne Cecilie brushed her hair back from her face. Ordinarily she wore a scarf, but she must have seen the two men talking and knew her brother needed help.

"Let me tell you something about Norwegians, Voldemar. If there is a storm at sea, every fisherman is well aware of the other boats. The men watch the water in every direction while they head for the safety of the harbor. No man ties his lines at the wharf and then goes home, if other boats are still out. Until every fisherman is safe, the village is not safe. Not just me and mine, Voldemar. All of us together."

"So we are," the young man answered, "on the Baltic."

"Ja. Now I could hear during rehearsals a great divergence between the tempo at which you kept trying to play, and the tempo that Johannes set for us."

"Tempo! The man has nothing but a dying pulse."

"All right, all right. Now listen. Johannes is out in the storm. He is alone on his boat, almost capsized in huge pounding waves. But we will help him to make it to the harbor. Even if one of us has to grab him out of the sea, we will haul him over the gunnel and then head to port." She looked up at the sky, silver-blue just minutes before sunrise. "The day promises to be a beauty. Arrangements have been made so that you and Johannes will spend it together. I guarantee, Voldemar," she glanced at her brother, as if for confirmation, "you will have your tempo tonight."

Voldemar studied her carefully. Then he seemed, for the first time since his arrival, to relax, slightly, placing an increment of trust in the people who had invited him to Oslo. "And when shall this meeting with the conductor take place?"

"Johannes will phone Per Olaf this morning. Then you and Maestro Berg can arrange where the two of you will meet. We will gladly drive you to wherever you need to go. Probably the concert hall."

"This morning. *Early* this morning?"

"Well, the cows aren't even milked yet. Let's say, if Johannes has not phoned us by nine o'clock, we'll give him a call."

"Eight o'clock. Please."

Now Per Olaf stepped into the discussion. "After breakfast, Voldemar, I'd like to take a walk with you to an old stone pile at the far end of the ridge." He pointed toward a nub of gray rock about a kilometer away, just visible, out in the open near the edge of the spruce forest. "It's a grave mound, five thousand years old, with somebody still inside it. Let's us two farmers go visit the first tillers of the soil in these parts. By the time we get back to the farmhouse, it'll be just about nine o'clock."

Voldemar emptied his cup of coffee, then held the cup in his two gloved hands. "All right. But I want Maestro Berg to understand that I do not come alone to this concert. I have been a polite little boy long enough."

"Maestro Berg," said Per Olaf, "the real Maestro Berg, would gladly help you to kick Joseph Stalin right in the teeth."

CHAPTER 4

Eli Margrethe awoke in a box, a box inside a city, but in her mind she could hear the waves washing against the rocks of her northern island. And she could hear as well a cello playing in the background, *basso continuo*. Sometimes that quiet cello would rise to the foreground and become a solo. Then it portrayed the majesty of an ocean wave, rolling toward her Lofoten Islands, at the very moment when the wave first caught the light of the sun rising over the jagged coastal mountains. The face of the wave became a palette of colors and glittering light, which the cello rendered with great dignity, while accompanied by flute, oboe, trumpet, and triangle. And the bassoon, turquoise descending into purple.

Then the cello would deepen, into the cold dark rolling depths of the wave, while a clarinet and piccolo played the white dancing froth on the ever-toppling crest.

Now, leaving *forte* for *pianissimo*, the cello returns to the background, letting human voices take over. A choir sings the old songs from the sea that her grandfather used to sing on his boat. The cello never stops in the background—the great wave never stops rolling—as the voices surge and quiet, surge and quiet, through five or six songs.

And then, growing out of a solo baritone, one last human voice calling from a boat far out at sea, the cello returns with a steady *crescendo* as the towering storm wave surges toward a fleet of fishing boats. The fishermen, who do not yet see the dark clouds, are setting their nets during the frigid night of January for the life-giving cod.

Now the storm, in the third section of the second movement. That was still to be written. Today, she would work with the songs.

And after the storm, the *Adagio* that finished the second movement . . . was something she was not yet ready to write. She was so

35

homesick, after six years buried in a city, struggling so hard to keep her spirits up, that she was not sure she could bear the anguish of that *Adagio*. As a girl, she had visited cemeteries along the coast where five, a dozen, sometimes more than twenty men— grandfathers, fathers, and sons, all of whom had drowned in the same storm—were buried. Or at least, if the body was never found, a stone had been erected. But that was too much sadness for her now. Her heart was already broken. Maybe this summer, with a vacation from the orchestra, she could go home and stand with her violin in a cemetery beside the sea, and let herself begin to hear the *Adagio*.

She loved the Tchaikovsky that she would play tonight, for the suffering, the anguish, and the grief in the first and last movements were so much more than just sadness. The suffering came when a person was not confronted, but overwhelmed, by a force before which he was utterly helpless. The anguish came from the love for everything that the person was losing. The greater the love, the greater the raging despair that life should be so abruptly and senselessly ended.

The grief came like brambles with thorns that overgrow an empty garden, filling it with a thicket of pain. A garden on shore, beside a house now empty of its husband and father. A house that sheltered a lone devastated mother, and hungry children.

Her own mother had been one of those children. The song that Mama still sang at the kitchen window for her father, while looking out to sea, would be the faint dying melody at the end of the *Adagio*.

Eli Margrethe opened her eyes and peered around her box, lit by morning sunshine through a single window. On the wall beyond the foot of her bed was a poster of Gunnar Berg's magnificent mountain, snow on jagged rock, towering over Svolvær Harbor. Outside her window, she could hear a trolley rolling heavily along the Majorstuen tracks. She ached to hear the cry of seagulls, the tumultuous squawks and shrieks of a gathering flock as the gulls fought—or celebrated—over fish guts tossed into Henningsvær Harbor by a fisherman cleaning his catch. During her six years in Oslo, she had ached every morning for the noise of those gulls. For the slap of a wave against the wharf pilings. For the voices of fishermen calling to each other from their decks as they prepared for the day's work.

Oh, give her a fisherman any day, and not these city boys. Six years with the café crowd. With talk about websites, and football games, and politics.

Ja, she had succeeded surprisingly well during the six years. She had obtained both a degree from the College of Music, and a job with the Symphony. Extraordinary success, really. But that was exactly the problem. The more successful she was in Oslo, with a job that she no doubt should keep for perhaps the rest of her life, the more trapped she became. What she really wanted was to be out on a chugging boat, a boat that smelled of engine oil and cod liver, listening to a fisherman's laughter as he told her some tale of a summer storm which he had weathered and weathered well. She wanted a man whose hair and skin and lips smelled of the sea. And she wanted her children to grow up by the sea. Not where people walk through a city park and look at ducks swimming in a pond.

Music was her gift, and her curse. At the age of three, she was already running her stubby fingers over the keys of her grandfather's piano. She was taking piano lessons at home before she had entered first grade at school. By the time she was eight, her father was driving her to weekly lessons in the big town of Svolvær. But when she was nine, she watched, she heard, Arve Tellefsen on television, and she knew it was not the piano but the violin that she should be playing. The high school in Svolvær loaned a violin to the little girl of nine. The weekly drives from Henningsvær to Svolvær continued, but now to the home of a violin teacher. A teacher who told her, when she was fourteen, that she would soon have to study in either Bergen or Oslo.

So music became her curse. What does a girl do with a God-given talent? Tell God that she doesn't want it?

She was two people, really. Or, almost three. She was an island girl, who loved to breathe the brine. She was a violinist, with a talent that had not yet stopped growing.

Inger Magnussen, the principal chair with the Oslo Symphony itself, had come to talk with her after a college concert. Inger had been able to pick out the voice of Eli Margrethe's violin, had watched Eli's bowing technique, had seen how closely the young woman followed the conductor. Inger came backstage after the concert. Following a few polite compliments, she invited Eli Margrethe to lunch. So they could talk. About an opening in the second violin section.

And Eli Margrethe was also, secretly, a composer. Only Astrid knew. Astrid would play the cello through the second movement, would render the waves that never cease in the background, the waves that sometimes rise to the foreground, beneath the birds, beneath the voices, beneath the grief.

Astrid was the only person who knew that Eli Margrethe was writing a three-movement symphony. That she had already completed the first movement, had started the second, and had written certain parts of the third: brief passages that portrayed the eagle, the puffins, and shimmering green curtains of northern lights.

She had started to write her symphony last October, when she was so homesick that she simply had to live for part of each day inside that world up north. She would become so absorbed for hours, penning notes and striking a quick line at the end of each measure, that afterwards, when she was making her solitary dinner, she realized how alive she had felt. The courses in counterpoint and orchestration at the College had helped enormously. She had known when she took them that one day she would like to write something. But she had no idea that her first work would pour out on the scale of oceanic waves and towering mountains. She had written much of the first movement right here in this box, at a small student desk, with tears running down her face. As happy as she had ever been in her life.

Music was her gift, and her curse. Today, all day Saturday, within the confines of Oslo, she would try to capture the voices of men and women singing to each other, and singing out to sea. Ja, she would work on the vocal section of the second movement. And she would hear, all through the day, beneath those voices, the cello which she was already hearing when she awoke: as if it had been playing while she was asleep and had continued to play, *basso continuo*, when the new day began. Astrid would be with her, so Eli was not entirely alone. Astrid gave her enough strength to keep listening to those voices, to keep writing them down.

Would she write today at the desk? She could not see any sky from her window, but the sunlight in the courtyard was very bright. And the air through the open window was certainly warm. Lifting her head to look at the foot of the bed, she saw that she had tossed away her eiderdown during the night. Spring at last.

Maybe she would take her violin and her notebook to a spot

outside where she could work. In a park. A quiet corner of a park. The quietest corner she knew, without taking a train somewhere, was behind the Royal Palace, on the little hill above a pond. Only a few people walking in and out of the adjoining neighborhood passed through that section of the park. Mothers with baby buggies on a Saturday morning.

Maybe someone might listen from an open palace window. Ja, maybe someone might listen on the first warm day of spring, to a violin playing the ancient songs of the loyal and loving citizens of the north.

CHAPTER 5

Lillian awoke in the deep warm darkness of her sleeping bag, her shoulder against Bjørn's shoulder. She stretched her legs and flexed her back; even with the camping pads, the pier was a hard bed. But the gorgeous man beside her . . . She could have slept with him on an ironing board all night, and still felt herself to be the most blessed woman in all the world.

When Bjørn was a little boy (Lillian knew this story by heart, and liked to think of it often, for it enabled her to know him all the way back to when he was a boy of five), the rain taught him how to play the drum. He had been born on the island of Sotra, southeast from Bergen. His house, in the village of Telavåg near the western coast of the island, faced the village harbor, a cleft in the granite island. Bjørn's bedroom window looked out at red and yellow houses ringing the long rocky harbor, and small fishing boats moored on buoys or tied to a dock. Sometimes, when the sun shone, the gray harbor turned a beckoning blue.

A short distance from the house was an old chicken coop, with weather-beaten walls and a brine-corroded tin roof, where his grandmother had kept chickens after the war. When Bjørn was just five, he was lying in bed one morning when he noticed not only the sound of rain on the tin roof outside the window, but the *changes* in the sound of rain beating on the metal: the first blasting batter of big rain drops when the storm hit the island; the enriching of the sound as the drops became smaller but more plentiful; the rising of the roar as the storm's fierce wind hit; the undulations, louder, softer, louder, softer, as the wind gusted and subsided. Bjørn did not realize how closely he was listening; he was only five. But he still remembers back to that morning as the first time.

A few years later, he was at his desk facing the window, doing his third grade homework (proper handwriting of a dozen selected sentences by Bjørnson), when a squall came sweeping across the sea from the southwest. Whereas most people would have closed the window, Bjørn had already, despite protests from both his mother and father, puttied four sheets of glass—the bottom and three sides of a long box—to the bottom of the window, so that he could leave the window open a full ten centimeters, even in a driving rainstorm. The glass box caught the water and drained it into juniper bushes below. Only a damp mist blew into the room, rising almost straight up from the inner wall of the wet box; the wind never disturbed the papers on his desk. So as the storm now blew across the sea toward his house, he did not close the window. He never, even during the worst gales of winter, closed the window anymore. He wanted to hear the rain.

But this time, he did not just listen to it.

He was only in third grade, but he could still remember today that the month was September, when evenings were getting dark early. That particular storm struck his window with a volley of hard pellets: corn snow, balls of ice. The pellets soon became big battering drops of rain. Waves of torrential rain drummed on the window, drummed on the tin roof, and spattered on the rocks.

He could hear three different pitches of drumming. Three entirely different sounds: window, roof, and rocks. The tin roof was the richest in overtones.

Without any special awareness of what he was doing, Bjørn began to drum with his fingertips on the edge of the pine table that served as his desk. As the volume of the roar of the rain increased outside, so did the volume of Bjørn's smooth steady drumming. He did not worry about his own sound, his own overtones; he just followed the steady drumming on the tin roof: louder, quieter, louder, quieter. His own drumming was so quiet that neither his mother nor his father heard him. He drummed for two or three minutes, until his arms grew tired.

Over the months, his arms grew stronger. In October, he made a drum with a goat hide stretched over one end of an old nail barrel. His parents *did* hear the noise now, so he swept out a corner of the chicken coop, opened a window on its rusty hinges (a window from which the chickens had once admired the harbor while they laid their eggs), then installed an old chair with a not too badly broken seat, and his goat-hide drum. Every rainy afternoon after school, the third-grader in the chicken coop drummed in tandem with the rain thundering overhead on the metal roof.

In good weather, he sat outside the chicken coop, bundled in wool, his drum braced at a slight angle between his knees. By the time summer arrived—the summer between third and fourth grade— his father had consented to buy (for his most unusual son) a conga drum in Bergen. The music shop had to order the conga from Oslo, which in turn ordered such instruments from Cuba. The Saturday in July when Bjørn and his father drove across the big suspension bridge from Sotra into Bergen to fetch the conga drum was, as Bjørn tells it, "the day I molted out of childhood and became who I really am."

Standing on a tripod of steel legs, the mahogany drum was nearly as tall as Bjørn. So he stood on a wooden box beside his drum in the chicken coop—a shorter box every year for the next three years—until as a seventh grader he not only needed no box, but he could drum for an hour easily through a cadence of home- made rhythms, with toughened hands and tireless arms and shoul- ders broader by far than the shoulders of any other boy in his class.

"Bjørn and his Cuban drum," his mother would say, marveling at this boundlessly energetic stranger who was a part of her family. When he was sixteen, his father finally got out the camera. Dad took a picture of his tall, lean, dark-haired son, facing the sea on a brilliant blue afternoon in June while he drummed on the mahogany conga (Dad took the picture from behind and to one side), as if Bjørn were sending a message to a sea goddess a kilometer away. Bjørn liked the picture and had an enlargement made; because his father's old camera had been set at one-thirtieth of a second, Bjørn's hands above the head of the conga were blurred.

At sixteen, he began lessons on a snare drum. Within a month, he joined the High School Music Corps as a drummer. He enjoyed marching with the band in the school parade on the Seventeenth of May. He thought of one day becoming a drummer in a rock band. Or of spending a summer in Cuba, with the real masters of the conga.

Then, during his final year of high school, he rode on the bus with the rest of the band into Bergen, where that evening they would hear the Bergen Symphony perform Igor Stravinsky's "The Rite of Spring." He had no idea what he was about to experience, despite his teacher's lecture describing the Russian composer and "new music." Mr. Bakken had gotten good seats for everyone in the band: fourteen seats in the front row, on the left side, only a few unimpeded meters from the musicians. Bjørn noticed, while the musicians were tuning their violins and horns, an arc of five copper timpani in the very back row of the orchestra. The drummer leaned down, with his ear almost touching the head of a drum, while he tapped with a felt-knobbed drumstick.

Then the conductor walked onto the stage. People applauded, the theater quieted, the conductor on the podium raised his arms above the silent musicians . . . and the music hit Bjørn like a tidal wave.

He was in it, inside the sound, aware of nothing else in all the universe. Although he listened for the kettledrums and followed them whenever they played, it was the power of a full symphony orchestra, not just a puny little school band, throbbing with Stravinsky's savage rhythms, that awakened him far more than puberty had yet done. Inside the sound, he was fully alive for the first time, hearing rhythms that he had never before known existed. He heard five separate pitches on the timpani, as the blur of drumsticks flew back and forth in absolutely perfect syncopation with the rest of the galloping orchestra. Sometimes the drums seemed to press the others on. Sometimes they supported, encouraged, coaxed along.

During those two mysterious, primeval, instinctual movements of the symphony, Bjørn the student became Bjørn the novice aching to become a real musician. When he walked with the other kids out of the concert hall and back to the bus, he understood that he had been to a different country, a different world, and he wanted to go back.

Now, twelve years later, Bjørn was Lillian's husband, and the two of them played with the Oslo Symphony, she on flute, he on his beloved timpani.

She was the luckiest woman alive, for he loved it when she massaged with coconut oil his gorgeous shoulders.

Lillian nudged on her back to the top of the sleeping bag, careful not to awaken Bjørn. Their two bags had been zipped together for the past ten years. She poked her head out into sunshine that made her squeeze her eyes shut. The air was surprisingly warm.

Reaching up with one hand from inside the bag, she pulled off her knit hat—they both wore knit hats on cool nights in their sleeping bags—and realized as she felt the fresh air on the top of her head that she had been sweating.

She opened her eyes, just a crack at first, and looked straight up at the most lovely blue sky. Rolling over onto her stomach, she saw the frozen lake beyond the end of the pier, and the green-black forest that wrapped around the lake. The ice looked soft. No skiers would cross the lake today. Not a soul around. How nice to sleep on the end of a pier as if the whole lake were their own, and to awaken on what seemed to be the first real day of spring.

Then she snuggled back down into the bag. If she pretended to be asleep, Bjørn would eventually wake up, try to kiss her awake, then get up and build a fire on shore and brew that first wonderful pot of coffee.

Bjørn felt Lillian stirring beside him, felt her nudge like a caterpillar to the top of her cocoon, then felt the caterpillar retreating back down into its cocoon. Lillian laid her arm over his chest, grabbing, as she always did, the muscle over his heart. Ja, he had married Stravinsky's nymph.

Her father had wanted to sacrifice her to law school. But Harriet, her father's mother, the real keeper of the scepter of power in the family, had insisted on music school. After all, the girl had been playing her grandmother's silver flute for twelve years, since her first airy peep at the age of six. And Harriet herself had been prevented by her husband from ever playing the flute outside the house. No man in the family was ever again going to hold back any woman in the family. Especially a young woman so clearly gifted.

Harriet had played the flute quite well within the confines of the stately Holmenkollen home. But Lillian, playing with the school orchestra, developed a clear, steady tone that lifted above the racket of the other instruments and sang its melody into the ear of every astonished member of the parental audience. In the spring of her last year in high school, three critics from three Oslo newspapers were in the auditorium when she performed first the treble part of Bach's "The Well-Tempered Clavier," accompanied by harpsichord; then Mozart's "Concerto in G" for flute, accompanied by two oboes, two

French horns, and strings; and finally, stunningly, her own composition for jazz flute and orchestra.

She played solo flute in the spotlight while the student orchestra struggled to keep up; it was, Harriet said after the concert, like "bats trying to follow an angel across the heavens." All three Oslo newspapers called her brilliant. Her dour curmudgeon of a father, covered with dust from the countinghouse, would have to look to one of his far less promising sons to become the family lawyer.

Bjørn placed his hand over Lillian's hand on his bare chest. She immediately snuggled closer to him, and hummed sleepily against his shoulder, as if to say Good Morning.

He had met Lillian at the College of Music, and a year later had married her with the determined and jubilant approval of Harriet, and despite the glum resistance of Morten the Rigid. The newlyweds spent their honeymoon—Harriet paid for the plane tickets and hotel—on the beaches and in the villages of Cuba.

Now, even ten years later, the other members of the orchestra called Lillian and Bjørn "the honeymooners." They were so deeply in love, always holding hands, secretly kissing when they thought no one was looking. And glancing at each other so often during rehearsals (Lillian would peer back over her shoulder) that Johannes would sometimes tap his baton at them. With a smile.

What Bjørn had become, what Lillian had become, in Cuba, was a revelation to the both of them: they grew as musicians, as man and woman, as citizens of the world. Their dreams, their *real* dreams, had been born in Cuba. For ten years, they had been building those dreams. As members of a symphony orchestra. As lovers in two well worn sleeping bags on warm and cool and snowy nights beneath the stars. And as . . . they did not know what yet; but somehow they were going to reach out to the people in the world who needed a little help.

Last night, for the first time in eleven years, Lillian was off the pill. With a doctor's counseling, and with a watchful eye on her womanly rhythms, she was ripe. They had had their ten years as honeymooners. Now, on the first non-wintry evening to present itself as a gift, an invitation, an urging, they had opened themselves to the possibility of a child. Of a family.

They had finished rehearsal on Friday evening—it had been an embarrassing session, struggling along with Johannes at his worst yet—then at home, Bjørn rolled up the sleeping bags while Lillian packed a picnic. They rode the trolley to Sognsvann, then followed the path at dusk beside the frozen lake to the first of two piers near its northern end. The gray boards were bare of snow, although a good amount of snow still remained unmelted in the forest. So they walked out to the end of the pier, inflated their mattresses, laid down their sleeping bags (with rolled-up sweaters for pillows), quickly undressed as the first stars were appearing, slid inside the hard bed, and celebrated their own Rite of Spring.

Now in the darkness of his sleeping bag, Bjørn lifted Lillian's hand from his chest and kissed her fingers. He asked her, "Whose turn to get up and make the coffee?" Her hand withdrew from his, then her finger poked him in the chest.

"All right." His backpack was on the pier; the old black pot was tied to it, and a bag of fresh coffee was in a pouch. His conga drums also lay on the pier, in their leather cases. Her backpack lay beside his; her flute was inside it. Not his best congas, of course. Not her best flute. His camping drums, her camping flute. Coffee, breakfast, and a picnic with Harriet. Then dinner in town at Vegeta Vertshus, the restaurant near the Concert House. Music all morning, music in the afternoon, an untiring duet. Then music tonight.

Maybe. If they could all agree on a *tempo*.

Bjørn wriggled in the sleeping bag until his head popped out into the sunshine. He lifted the knit hat from over his eyes, blinked at the yellow sun already above the trees: the tip of the pier was in sunlight, the rest still in shadow.

He reached down into the bag, found Lillian's hand, pulled her hand out of the bag and again kissed her fingers. She rubbed her fingertips over the stubble on his cheek. Then her hand disappeared back into the bag, as if some giant sea creature had withdrawn its tentacle.

He wriggled out of the bag and stood up, his bare feet on the smooth warm boards of the pier. The only thing he had been wearing was the knit hat against the chill of the night. Now, without even a hat, he stood with the sun warm on his back while he stared at the soft, gray-white ice that covered the lake.

As he had always savored that first moment when a storm's driving rain hit his window, so he now savored the first moment of spring: before any haze of green appeared on the white birch trees along the opposite shore; before any glint of sunshine sparkled on open water; before even the first duck had returned.

It was the first morning, the first heartbeat, of spring.

Today, on drums, on flute, they would play a jubilant duet of Welcome.

Part II

A Greater Sin Than War

CHAPTER 6

After a congenial breakfast, and before the expected phone call, Per Olaf took Voldemar for a walk to the old grave mound. While they followed a broad grassy ridge toward the corner of the spruce forest, Per Olaf felt the warm morning sun on his face. Sweeping his eyes across rolling brown land, he knew that today was the day the sun would warm the earth enough that the seeds would awaken. Today, the seeds would begin to stir.

Voldemar walked beside Per Olaf, sweeping his own eyes across the land, and up at the celestial blue sky. Per Olaf was pleased to see that Voldemar walked like a farmer, with confident strides across the uneven ground. Voldemar wore a white shirt and black trousers; no overcoat, no suit coat, no gloves. His hands, after the long winter, were pale.

Murphy rambled ahead of them, delighted with an early morning walk. He had managed to scare up a rabbit, which bounded off at twice Murphy's shambling speed.

Per Olaf could hear a vague bit of melody in his mind, something ethereal and beautiful, but he had too much to think about now to pursue it. After a talk with old Hulda and Torstein, they needed a phone call from Johannes.

Neither Per Olaf nor Voldemar felt any need to speak as they traversed the ridge, the dark edge of the spruce forest to their right, pasture and distant potato fields dropping downhill to their left. They walked about a kilometer, to the first corner of the spruce woods, where the line of trees angled to the right, and the ridge flattened, broadened, into a large pasture nearly ringed by spruce. The pasture was empty of cows now, for the herd was not yet back from the barn.

Just outside the corner of the spruce woods, as if one footstep into the pasture, stood a grassy mound of rocks about five meters tall. Per Olaf kept the burial mound and the ring of grass around it well cleared of any saplings. Old Hulda and Torstein had been farmers who cleared the land and planted their seed. Their grave must never be overrun by trees. They must rightfully sleep in their well-tended pasture.

"My wife Ingeborg," said Per Olaf, "calls the old couple inside the mound Hulda and Torstein. Or at least, we imagine an old couple to be inside. We don't want to disturb them to find out."

"Hmmm," said Voldemar. "We have such graves. Ancient."

"Maybe," said Per Olaf, "your first people and my first people were farming at about the same time."

"Hmmm," said Voldemar.

They stood together, facing the people from five thousand years ago. Per Olaf heard the wind toss through the spruce behind them. Wind from the southwest, which almost never stopped blowing. Wind from the fjord, somersaulting up the hills along the coast, then sweeping across the hilltops.

"You know, Voldemar, a man comes to love his land."

Voldemar looked at him and nodded, inviting more.

"When I was a young soldier, putting in my required time, I was stationed way up above the polar circle on the tundra, near a town called Kautokeino. In the autumn, the heath on the tundra becomes the most brilliant orange and red. The birch become bright yellow. On a day in September—on a clear day like today—the sun sharpens those colors, makes them vibrant." Per Olaf paused, remembering colors so vivid that he had to savor them for a moment. "The land rolls like a vast quilt beneath an immense blue sky, rolls in every direction toward the ends of the earth." He added, warmed by the many friendships in his heart, "That's the land of the Sami, the reindeer people."

Murphy had started to dig. He had found a good spot in the pasture. His claws ripped up the brown grass, reached for the black soil beneath.

Per Olaf continued, "I had brought my trumpet with me to the north, so that when I was off duty, I might practice, keep up my lip. One Sunday afternoon, a gorgeous afternoon in September, I took my horn with me when I started off on a hike across the tundra. I wore rubber boots, and a sweater that was almost too warm, and I carried my trumpet in its case.

"I came to a lake, narrow but fairly long, ringed with a rocky shore. A few scattered birch grew in that area, none more than four meters tall. Slender white trunks rose above the scarlet blaze of the heath. I found a fairly flat boulder, set the case on it and took out my trumpet. I wanted to send a fanfare out over that long, narrow lake, wanted to play notes as vibrant as the colors, as clear as the air, as sharp as the sparkles on the wind-rippled water."

Per Olaf wondered for a moment if he might be able to take a trip north this coming September.

"I had been playing a good long time—with nobody around that I might be bothering, you see—when I heard someone singing, a man's voice, distant. I turned the bell of my trumpet toward the sound, for I did not want to stop playing, and spotted a man walking along the opposite edge of the lake. He was singing a melody unlike any melody I had ever heard before. I quieted my playing, so that I could better hear him."

Per Olaf paused, hearing again that intriguing Sami *yoik*.

"The bell of my trumpet followed the man as he walked along the opposite shore. The lake was perhaps fifty meters across, so I could hear him quite well. He wore no bright Sami colors, no blue and red of Kautokeino, but simply brown. His face was turned toward me, toward the sound of my trumpet. He seemed to be singing to the lake while he walked along her shore.

"I tried to follow his melody, or the drift of his melody, or at least the strange harmonies within that melody, and finally found a B-flat that resonated. I played for him a *basso continuo*, a sustained note broken into rhythms and occasional riffs. I sent my music straight across the lake as he, always walking steadily, sent his song straight across the lake, so that I heard him, and he heard me, and our voices merged perfectly over the heart of the lake.

"The Sami kept walking (he never waved, and neither did I) along the far shore of the lake. He walked down a long orange and red hill, until he disappeared into a fluttering yellow woods. I stopped playing; I held my trumpet for a long time, then put it back into its case. I had to be back on duty in an hour and a half. But that mattered little. For I had just stood in a moment of human eternity."

Per Olaf stared across the pasture and felt the wind on his face. A breeze really, but almost always blowing. And certainly blowing up there, fifty meters above the ground. A wind from the sea blew over the land, offering power. Offering peace.

"You know, Voldemar, when the air gets dirty, the world gets warmer. I've read about it. Glaciers melting. Water rising in the Pacific, so that already people are forced off their islands. In a matter of time, the tundra will begin to melt. The permafrost deep in the earth: it will melt. The snow will change: it will be wetter snow. Not the perfect cold dry snow that people and reindeer can so easily travel on. And then what happens? Voldemar, coal is killing the tundra. Gasoline is killing the tundra. We have already started the first faint nudge toward Getting Too Warm. And once the melting begins, we're surely not going to be able to stop it. There will be no technical fix. Then what happens to the Sami and their reindeer? What happens to people who deeply love their land?"

Voldemar stared at him with his dark intent eyes, listening.

Per Olaf continued, "Your country and my country have both suffered from the ravages of war. Yours more than mine. But Voldemar, there is a greater sin than war. That sin is the slow killing of our earth."

Per Olaf pointed to the middle of the pasture. "Do you know what I want to do? Out there in the grass and wildflowers where a hundred cows graze, I want to build a wind turbine. A white tubular tower in the blue sky, fifty meters tall, with three long white blades. Blades that spin with slow steady grace. Pumping electricity to a dozen farms. To a hundred farms."

He liked to imagine the turbine automatically facing its blades into the wind, automatically adjusting the pitch of the blades to the strength of the wind.

"But more than that. A wind turbine would be a monument. Like the towering steeple of a cathedral back in the year Twelve Hundred. A monument announcing a new spirit in the land. A new and deeper understanding. A monument affirming a better time to come."

Per Olaf took a deep breath of the wind on his face, then blew it out slowly.

"I already have electricity from a river: clean power that does not spread filth upon the air. Nevertheless, I would like to stand such a monument on my land, where old Hulda and Torstein can watch those big white blades turning so majestically, powering light bulbs and milking machines in the barn, powering the coffee maker in the kitchen, powering my old record player and the new CD player. Powering Ingeborg's computer. A monument to what we could do, if we would only let ourselves do it."

Per Olaf felt the anger rising in him. "We are six billion fools. Because a greater sin than war is the sin of killing the earth."

"Hmmm," said Voldemar. He looked at his watch. "Maybe we should start back?"

The phone call from Johannes. Voldemar did not want to miss it.

As they walked back along the ridge, the red barn in the distance stood like books between the bookends of the two white houses. Per Olaf heard in his mind that faint melody again. Something by Sissel Kyrkjebø. He couldn't remember the words, only a wisp of a melody, and the sad yet strong tone of her voice.

Then he heard Voldemar saying to him, "My parents still live on the farm, and we have talked about a wind turbine. But not, primarily, to protect the earth. We would like a wind turbine—a thousand wind turbines across Estonia—so that we do not have to depend on any other country for oil. Especially, Russian oil. We want our own turbines, our own electricity. Our own future."

"Ja," said Per Olaf. Power and peace. From that giant daisy with three white petals, spinning in the wind.

Then he could stand beside the burial mound, with old Hulda and Torstein, facing the turbine out in the pasture. He would play with the bell of his trumpet lifted into the wind, wind that had passed through those tireless wings. He would play a fanfare. He would have to write a new one. For a new age, a new Renaissance. When the Earth could be her old healthy self again, and people could continue their long trek at slowly becoming something better than what they had been.

The two men walked past the garden fence, heard a faint voice and then laughter in the barn. They climbed the three broad steps onto the porch of Per Olaf's house, then they paused. Both men turned around for a last look back at the land: at the long brown ridge where they had walked, at the gray nub of rock a kilometer away, at the descending hills to the left of it, at the distant fringe of spruce along the horizon. And at the pure blue sky overhead.

The morning sun shone warmly on their faces. From its height,

Per Olaf gauged the hour to be about eight-thirty. Voldemar turned toward the door, ready to go inside. He didn't want to miss the phone call from Johannes.

CHAPTER 7

After he hung up the phone, Voldemar explained to Per Olaf, his wife Ingeborg, and his sister Anne Cecilie (all of whom had sat at the kitchen table while he had spoken on the phone), that the concertmaster had invited him to go sailing with the conductor. They would go over the score while they were aboard a sailboat on the fjord. They would have all afternoon to go over the music.

"That's a good plan," said Per Olaf.

"I'll put together a basket of food for lunch," said Anne Cecilie.

"I shall help," said Ingeborg.

"Ja," said Per Olaf.

Voldemar told them, "The concertmaster suggested that I wear something warm. She said the wind on the fjord could sometimes be surprisingly cold."

Per Olaf stood up from the kitchen chair, disappeared into his bedroom, and soon came out with a faded blue shirt and a pair of jeans wrapped over his arm, on top of two sweaters: one light, one for winter. "Try these on," he said.

Voldemar took the clothing to his own bedroom (the room had once belonged to a now-grown son). He took off the white shirt and black slacks which he had unfolded from his suitcase that morning, and put on the old clothes that were long enough, though a bit roomy in the waist. He uncoiled Per Olaf's old brown belt, ran it through the loops on the jeans, pulled it snug. Good enough.

Then he opened his briefcase, took out his piano score and lay it on the flowery bedspread beside the sweaters. He was ready. He hoped the conductor would be ready too.

When he returned to the kitchen, he saw that Ingeborg and Anne Cecilie were filling two baskets with jars and cans and loaves of bread. "I think I'll wait outside," he said to them.

Both of the women looked at him; both nodded that the clothes were a good fit.

"Fine," said Anne Cecilie. "It'll take about an hour for them to drive from Oslo. Per Olaf's in the barn with Odd."

"Hmmm."

Voldemar stepped out into the sunshine, crossed the yard to the fence around a big rectangular garden, and stood with his hands on the top railing. Back home, he would have taken off the blue denim shirt, to feel the sun on his chest. But here he was a guest, and had best be a bit formal.

He was beginning to believe that he would actually meet with Johannes Berg, would have time to go over the score before the concert tonight. That they would do so on a sailboat was fine. If the boat was anything like Anu's boat, he would be right at home with the sails and lines.

He was beginning to believe that maybe there would be a successful concert. That he would, as he had planned with Anu for months, send home an unprecedented concert that all of Estonia would hear. She would see to that, for she worked as assistant station manager at Radio Tallinn. For this one program, they had promoted her to station manager: she was in charge of the broadcast. Over the past few weeks, she had emailed and phoned Edvard, the sound manager with the Oslo Symphony, a dozen times, working out every last detail. The concert would be transmitted by satellite to Tallinn, where Anu would send it out to the nation. She was as nervous as he was. But she had no idea of all that he had been through during this past horrendous week in Oslo.

Never mind. Maybe there would be a successful concert after all. His parents and Anu's parents would be together, out on her family's sailboat, with the battery-powered radio, listening to the music while they swung at anchor. By nine o'clock on an April evening, the night would be dark. No moon tonight, only stars. Very clear stars, if the weather held. Too bad that Anu had to be in the studio in Tallinn.

He leaned against the fence, felt the rail press against his waist, cupped his hands over the rough wood. Then he heard his mother's voice, singing one of the hundreds of songs that she knew. Songs that had kept his people alive for eight hundred years. And for how many thousands of years before that? Songs that were stronger than Stalin. Songs that carried his people through a half century of Soviet brutality, until finally the Singing Revolution began.

It began, actually, without singing. It began with a love for the earth. In the spring of 1987, a few Estonians demonstrated in the streets of Tallinn against a phosphate mining project northeast of the city, an ugly and poisonous catastrophe managed by the authorities in Moscow.

Whether or not anyone in Moscow noticed, those few brave Estonians noticed each other.

On August 23 of that same year, another demonstration took place in Tallinn: thousands of people from throughout the country assembled to denounce the Molotov-Ribbentrop Pact of 1939, an agreement in which Hitler had handed Estonia, Latvia, and Lithuania to Stalin, in return for, first of all, Poland.

Once again, people were encouraged by the growing number of citizens in the streets.

In April of 1988, during a demonstration in the university town of Tartu, flags with horizontal blue, black, and white stripes appeared above the crowd, for the first time since 1940.

And then in June of 1988, when Voldemar was eight years old, a hundred thousand Estonians gathered at Tallinn's outdoor theater for a song festival. A huge concrete concert shell, which cupped over a broad stage of rising steps, faced an enormous sloping lawn. The tilted stage could hold a choir of thirty thousand singers. The audience, seated on the grass, was able to look beyond the stage at the blue Gulf of Finland behind it. Voldemar's father and mother had brought him by train from their village to the city of Tallinn. It was the first such festival—a festival bound to become a demonstration of some sort—which his family had dared to attend.

Voldemar was overwhelmed by the great number of people gathering on the vast lawn. He gripped his father's hand, so not to be lost in the seething crowd. He was proud of his father and mother for having brought the family to something of such importance.

Then the singing began, as thousands of singers on the stage, amplified by the huge shell behind them, sent their voices out to an audience that knew the words to every song. No Russian folk tunes this time. No Soviet marching songs. These songs, this music, was purely Estonian. It was as if, after eight centuries bound in chains in a dungeon, where quiet voices had sung one by one, and sometimes two by two, the soul of Estonia had now slipped off the chains and thrown open the barred door, then climbed the dungeon steps toward an upper door, and the sunshine outside. Or at least, a glimpse of sunshine. For in 1988, Soviet tanks could still roll into Tallinn at any moment.

The voice of the enormous choir, the vibrant voice of thousands of brave people, sent verse after verse, song after song, through the hearts of a hundred thousand listeners. Voldemar felt his father's excitement, his mother's joy, saw tears on their cheeks. He understood, even at eight, that something very good was happening in his country.

The first music that he really heard, despite his piano lessons, despite the choir at school, was the voice of his nation, for now the people around him stood up from the grass and sang with voices that trembled when the load of love became unbearable. He heard his father singing, heard his mother singing, and discovered that he too knew most of the words, just by being around his mother's mother, who always sang while she knitted. As Voldemar joined his voice with the vast, rich, powerful voice that lifted from the great lawn and rose up to the blue summer sky, he knew that no matter what he did with his life, he would do it for his people.

In September of 1988, Estonians gathered for another song festival. This time his mother's parents came with them.

On January 18, 1989, Estonians declared that their national language would be Estonian.

On August 23, 1989, the Baltic peoples of Estonia, Latvia, and Lithuania held hands across their three countries in a chain of people almost six hundred kilometers long. Voldemar and his family were a part of that courageous gathering. He was now nine years old, holding hands with people in a line that stretched to Tallinn in one direction, and to Riga, and Vilnius, in the other. He understood that all three states were demanding their freedom from the Soviet Union.

On March 11, 1990, Lithuania declared its independence.

On January 13, 1991, Soviet soldiers killed Lithuanian citizens in Vilnius, and thereby threatened every measure of progress so far.

On March 3, 1991, Estonians voted in a referendum on the question of independence: 78 percent voted Yes. Those who voted No were Russians living in Estonia, Russians with no home in Russia to go home to.

On August 19, 1991, a Communist coup in Moscow caused a brief period of turmoil.

The next day, August 20, 1991, while Russian tanks fired on the Russian parliament, Estonians declared themselves to be free.

The next day, August 21, Latvia too declared itself independent.

On the next day, August 22, Iceland recognized both Estonia and Latvia.

On the next day, August 23, Norway and Denmark recognized all three new Baltic nations.

On August 29, Sweden opened an embassy in Tallinn.

On September 2, the United States recognized the three new Baltic nations.

On September 6, the Soviet Union quietly acknowledged the three declarations of independence.

And on September 17, 1991, all three Baltic nations joined the United Nations. In less than a month, from August 19 to September 17, Estonia had moved out of the Soviet Union and into the United Nations. Voldemar was eleven, and felt that he held hands with people all the way around the world.

Now he was twenty-three; he had lived his teenage years during his country's first decade of freedom. He and his country had grown with irrepressible vigor, and so had his talent. At the age of sixteen, he had entered the Estonian Music Academy, where he devoured every lecture, practiced night after night until midnight.

He met Anu at the Academy during a student recording session. She had believed in him from the first time she heard him play. She was his bedrock.

He made his debut with the Estonian National Symphony Orchestra when he was nineteen, playing Grieg's "A-Minor Piano Concerto." He loved the Grieg, and wanted to play something from a country which had never conquered Estonia. Beethoven would come later.

So as he stood now in the warm morning sunshine in Norway, waiting for the conductor to arrive, waiting for his own rehearsal to finally begin, he began to sing. He sang one after another of his mother's songs, of his grandmother's songs. Looking beyond the fenced garden, he sang his songs to the rolling farmland, to the brown earth basking in the sun, to old What's-Her-Name and What's-His-Name who lay buried in the grey mound of rock at the far end of the ridge.

He sang new songs too, patriotic songs about freedom. Lifting his face toward the southeast, he sang these brave songs not to the nearby hills, but to his country far across the sea.

He saw the dark blue car coming up the driveway, recognized the driver as the concertmaster. Looking carefully through the car's open window, he spotted the conductor in the passenger seat.

His singing for an hour had emptied him of anger. It had cleansed him of any bitter clinging to the past, and prepared him to grapple with the future. That was the power of a Singing Revolution.

He was ready.

CHAPTER 8

Inger followed the E6 south of Oslo, and could have taken the tunnel at Vinterbro, the shorter way to Per Olaf's house, but turned instead onto the E18, which also ran south, but stayed out in the sunshine. Anyway, she liked to drive through the village of Ås, as her father had always done. And she liked to drive past the agricultural college on the western edge of Ås, with its stately brick buildings and huge, ancient chestnut trees.

Johannes rode in silence, turning his head occasionally to look out the side window at the brown farm land.

Inger began to hum a song, one of her favorites: she could hear Sissel's voice singing quietly with just a piano in the background. The words were about sadness, or getting beyond sadness, but she didn't want the words just now. Humming the music, she felt its reassurance, its quiet beauty.

They drove through Ås, busy on a Saturday morning; drove past the college, deserted. Then they descended a long gentle hill and drove across an overpass over the E6. She glanced to the left: the divided highway stretched south all the way to Sweden.

Now they were on a lovely country road, route 152, winding between broad stretches of rolling farmland. Some of the fields were plowed, and some were covered with winter-flattened brown grass. Handsome farmhouses flanked the road, sheltered in copses of bare chestnut and maple. She drove down a long steep hill with a curve to the left, then she slowed—remembering Per Olaf's instructions on the phone—as she approached a country lane that headed left, south. She turned onto the lane; once again she was driving into the morning sun.

The lane dipped into a wooded valley, crossed a stream, then rose through the trees and emerged onto a broad open ridge. She spotted the mailbox on the right, slowed and hooked into Per Olaf's long gravel driveway. Two rows of maple trees, flanking the driveway, formed an arch of bare branches overhead.

She saw two white houses flanking a red barn; Per Olaf's house was on the left, he had told her.

She looked at Johannes, who was looking at her.

"Shall I apologize to Voldemar?" he asked. "Or shall we just have a fresh start?"

"An apology is in order," she said. "Then you'll have your fresh start."

"Ja."

No one was out on the porch of either house. No one was working outside of the barn. Then she noticed—she and Johannes both noticed at the same moment and turned their heads together—that Voldemar was standing alone beside a garden fence. He was wearing a blue denim shirt and blue jeans, from Per Olaf no doubt. He would need a sweater too, for the wind could turn cold out on the fjord.

Voldemar was watching them as they drove up the driveway. As she slowed to a stop in front of Per Olaf's farmhouse, she could hear through her open window that Voldemar was singing.

CHAPTER 9

Johannes saw three things at the same time, as he often heard three or five or a dozen different sounds while he was conducting, all of them clearly. He saw Voldemar walking toward the car, which had come to a stop in front of a white farmhouse. He saw, behind Voldemar, the gnarled black branches of an apple orchard. And he saw a big dog that came running from the farmhouse porch, a dog which, galloping now past the car window, was the filthiest dog he had ever seen in his life. The creature was black with dirt, even to the top of its head.

Johannes looked again through the windshield at Voldemar, and felt both a pang of shame for having let the boy down so horribly during the past week, and a tiny bit of relief, of gratitude, for the Estonian was smiling at him. Johannes opened the door and stepped out of the car into the sunny farmyard, then he walked directly toward his guest pianist.

"Voldemar." Johannes reached out his hand. "I want to apologize for what has been a very unprofessional week."

Voldemar took his hand and gripped it firmly. "Maestro Berg, in my country, with our history, we often say, 'Well, let's get started again.'"

Johannes saw the earnestness in the young man's eyes, a fierce readiness to turn to the music itself. The Estonian was a professional. No clutter, no grudges. We work.

"Ja," said Johannes. "Thank you."

The two hands squeezed firmly, broke apart comfortably. For both men, the day had begun.

Now Voldemar turned to Inger, who stood near them. "Is it true," he asked, "that we are going sailing?"

"A shake-down cruise," warned Inger, raising a finger of caution. "*If* the motor works well enough to get us out of the harbor. *If* the sails and lines are in good shape. *If* the hull hasn't sprung a leak during the winter."

Voldemar shrugged. "I am no good with motors. But give me a sail and lines, and I'll tune your sloop to the wind as if the vessel were a violin."

"Good," said Inger with a smile of gratitude. "I think you'll find a perfect wind out on the fjord today."

Per Olaf and his wife Ingeborg appeared on their porch. Johannes heard a door open behind him; he turned and saw Anne Cecilie on the porch of the second farmhouse.

Her husband Odd appeared from the side of the barn. Everyone was gathering to witness, and wish well, the meeting of conductor and pianist. Per Olaf and Ingeborg each carried a basket. Anne Cecilie carried a smaller basket. Odd carried a white liter bottle in each hand. There would clearly be enough food on this voyage, and milk.

Now the filthy dog went roaring past again. It began to circle the group of seven, orbiting them with joyful energy. Johannes could see bits of grass and ferns matted in the dog's fur.

Following a minute or two of cordial conversation (during which the concert that night was never mentioned), Inger asked Voldemar, "Do you have your suit ready? And your score?"

"Suit, score, two extra sweaters, and knit cap. Ingeborg thinks we're sailing to the North Pole."

"Ja," said Ingeborg, with a fond smile toward her guest. "You can't sit someone half-frozen down at the piano tonight."

"What about gloves?" asked Per Olaf. "Voldemar, you had gloves on this morning. Do you want them out on the water?"

Voldemar looked at Inger for advice. "Why not bring them?" he asked.

"I've got sailing gloves for everyone, but they're for gripping lines, not for warmth. Bring whatever you think you'll need to be warm on a day at sea in early April."

Voldemar stepped out of the group, crossed the farmyard to Per Olaf's house and hopped up the steps to the porch. They could hear him singing as he opened the door and disappeared inside.

Inger gratefully accepted the baskets of food and put them in the trunk of her car. She wrapped the two bottles of milk in a towel, stuffed them snugly upright between two baskets.

Johannes stared at an ancient black apple tree in an orchard beyond the fenced-in garden. He remembered lines of poetry from somewhere,

> "Let me believe as does the apple tree,
> So old in winter, so young in spring,
> For it never doubts the earth."

He wondered where he had left his baton. On the podium at the end of rehearsal on Friday? Or somewhere in his cluttered office?

Voldemar came out the door with a suit bag and two sweaters heaped over one arm, an old leather briefcase in his other hand, and a blue wool cap on his head. "Ready!" he called.

"Johannes," said Inger quietly, concertmaster to maestro, "do you mind riding in the back seat?"

"Fine," said Johannes. He stepped quickly to a rear door and got into the car, so the sailors could discuss the wind and lines and the cut of their sails.

The two in blue got into the front seats, closed their doors, and then everyone inside waved to everyone outside. Per Olaf called to the dog, "Murphy!" Murphy stopped orbiting and obediently sat, like a small woolly mammoth, beside Per Olaf.

Inger drove in a slow circle around the farmyard to the driveway, tooted her horn, then drove between the long twin rows of giant maples, each tree at least a century old, to where the driveway opened onto the paved country lane.

She turned left. Johannes sat back in his seat, opened a window. If the others in the orchestra were as gracious as Anne Cecilie and Per Olaf had been, and if everyone was as ready to go to work as this exuberant Voldemar, then there might possibly be a concert tonight.

For Johannes would not be the only passenger aboard ship today. Beethoven would be aboard too.

CHAPTER 10

As Inger drove down a series of hills toward the coast, she left behind the peaceful open farmland and entered the commercial outskirts of Drøbak. Her two passengers were quiet as they rode, waiting for their work together, on her sailboat. She glanced into the rearview mirror at Johannes: he was watching with interest a bicycle rider pedaling down the last long hill into the village. The man in a red helmet traveled almost as fast as her car while she slowly passed him. Johannes watched the man pumping his knees just outside the passenger window.

Johannes looked peaceful, content, ready for whatever came next. Ja, he certainly needed some sun on his face.

She felt a sharp pang of fear, with its twin, a deep sadness. Afraid to lose him, and already grieving because she had. That was the danger of ever thinking seriously about a man.

The village of Drøbak was busy on Saturday morning; the square was filled with a flea market. Wary of pedestrians, Inger followed a narrow lane down the last bit of hill to the harbor. Glancing out at the docks, she spotted Martin in a red shirt on the deck of the *Kristine Marie*, the sloop her father had named after her mother.

May he have the motor running, she thought.

But even if Martin could not get it going on this first day after the long winter (he might need parts, a hose or something), she could surely find somebody to tow the sloop from its berth in the harbor out to the fjord, where she could open her sails. She had to get her men to Oslo, six hours north. Motor or no motor, they had to reach the Oslo wharf by seven o'clock at the latest.

She parked behind the aquarium, stepped out of the car into the warm sunshine, walked to the edge of the wharf and stared out at the broad blue fjord: its rolling water was driven by a good strong wind from the south. She glanced at sailboats up and down the long

69

fjord: their sails were leaning. Good wind everywhere.

All she had to do was deliver her two men in proper shape for the concert tonight. At eight o'clock in the evening, the real Johannes had to be standing on his podium. And Voldemar had to have lightning in his hands. If she could do that—deliver them in shape and on time—then *there* would be a foundation that she and Johannes could build on. Never mind the sadness and the fear. Never mind the schoolgirl flutters. Today she was captain, and tonight she was concertmaster; matters of the heart could follow in due course.

Captain and crew carried baskets and suit bags across the parking lot and then along the pier that led out to her sloop. Halfway along the pier, she could hear the *Kristine Marie* chugging quietly. Martin stood on the bow with his back to her, coiling a line.

"Thank you, Martin," she called.

He turned around and gave her the handsomest grin she had ever seen on a man of eighty. "Purrs like a kitten, she does."

She glanced at the sloop's oaken hull, one of the few now among the many white fiberglass hulls. The *Kristine Marie* was slower than the others, and the maintenance was always a bit more, but every time Inger boarded the old boat, she could feel her mother's spirit, and her father's spirit, on the vessel with her. She wanted no other sloop; she would no doubt sail this boat until the day someone put her into the Drøbak nursing home.

She led her crew onto the narrow side dock flanking the sloop. As each man stepped aboard, she introduced him, "Martin, I would like you to meet Voldemar Keskküla, from Tallinn. And Johannes Berg, from Oslo."

Martin shook Voldemar's hand and said to him in English, "Welcome to Norway!"

"Takk," said Voldemar, the first word in Norwegian that Inger had heard him speak.

Johannes set his basket down on the stern deck, then he shook hands with Martin. "From Narvik, actually."

After Inger had stepped from the dock to the gunnel, to the bench, to the cockpit deck, Martin asked her, "How's my girl?" He had always been more than her parents' best friend: he was like a beloved uncle. He gave her a hug, and delighted her, as always, with his whiskery cheek.

She had phoned Martin yesterday evening to ask if he could

walk down to the harbor this morning to start the sloop's motor. Martin had worked for most of his life on trawlers, down in the engine room; he could listen to a motor the same way that she listened to her violin. Even when the sailboat's motor just growled and smoked, as it often did in the spring, Martin would listen to the way it growled, tinker with a spark plug or an air intake, then grin at her when the motor roared to life. Her father had never needed any other mechanic, and now, even ten years after Daddy was gone, Martin checked on the boat several times during the winter, and waited for her to name the day when the sloop should be ready for its first sail in the spring.

During the next twenty minutes, Martin showed Inger the steadily chugging motor, the radio, a wooden block at the top of the mast that would soon need replacing, while Johannes and Voldemar brought the rest of the gear from the car.

Then Johannes and Martin stood together in the stern while Inger and Voldemar brought up the sail bags from the locker in the bow, pulled out the sails, and, working efficiently together, fitted the mainsail to the mast and boom, then the jib to the forward shroud. Inger readied the starboard jib sheet, Voldemar the port sheet. Since the wind was from the south, and the *Kristine Marie* lay in her slip with her bow to the south, Inger briefly raised the mainsail and let it gently flap, so she could inspect it for wear and mold. The sails and lines were in excellent shape.

Martin stepped onto the dock, then he unfastened the four lines from their cleats. He cast each neatly coiled line onto the sloop's oaken deck. As Inger motored slowly forward out of the slip, he called to her, "I shall be in the concert hall tonight."

"Good," she called back. Martin still sat in the front row and a little to the left, directly facing her, where he had sat until ten years ago with her parents. Strangers now filled the two seats beside him. She added, "Be sure you come see me backstage after the concert."

"Ja," he laughed, "if I can afford the roses."

She spun the wheel, ruddering toward the mouth of the harbor.

"Give it more throttle," called Martin, his voice thin in the distance.

She throttled to a bit more power, heard the engine run more smoothly, felt her craft glide through the smooth clear water of the harbor toward the rolling blue water of the fjord.

Glancing back a last time, she waved to the tiny figure in a red shirt on the end of the pier. Thank you, Martin, she thought. The entire orchestra most gratefully thanks you.

Voldemar stood on the forward deck near the mast, ready to grab the halyard and hoist the main. Never could Inger have imagined, when she had debated with herself last night about whether or not to take the conductor and pianist out on her boat, that she would be blessed with a real sailor for crew.

She had a young Neptune on board. Together, they were going to do some fine sailing.

After she had motored a hundred meters from the mouth of the harbor, she glanced one last time across the fjord, south to north, alert for any threatening traffic. Then she called forward to Voldemar, "Hoist the main!" Up went her first white wing as he pulled on the line with his strong arms. He secured the halyard; she drew in the sheet and ran with the wind off her port quarter. She loved that moment when the deck tilted beneath her feet.

"Hoist the jib!" she called. Up went her second white wing. Voldemar secured the halyard; then he drew in the starboard sheet and secured it in a jam cleat, not too loose, not too tight.

She cut off the engine. In the silence that followed (like the silence that follows the clamorous tuning of the orchestra), she heard (like the first measures of music at the first strokes of the conductor's baton) water rushing along the hull, and the shrill welcoming cry of a gull.

CHAPTER 11

Astrid sat with her cello before her favorite audience. It always took about half an hour for the nurses to assemble the horseshoe of wheelchairs, and to help those who could still walk to find a seat. Her mother sat in a wheelchair right in the middle of the front row: the best seat in the house. Magnus sat beside her on a folding chair, his hand on her armrest, her hand on top of his. They spoke and laughed with each other, for her mother could still hear quite well. Mama was certainly the healthiest ninety-five-year-old in the nursing home. Had it not been for her fall on the ice and broken hip last January, she would still be at the old farmhouse up the mountain, talking to her goats. She had taken the move to the home bravely enough, especially because now her daughter played a solo concert every Saturday morning on the cello.

When everyone was assembled (some of them were already asleep in their chairs), Astrid began to play. She played an old children's song about a lamb, and saw faces turn toward her with a look of recognition. She played it through a second time, a little louder. A woman wearing a yellow bib began to tap her hand on her lap. Astrid played the happy song about the lamb a third time through, then she flowed, descending down the scale with a brief *arpeggio* to another key, to a song about chickens.

Astrid played a dozen old songs, some for children, some for people in love; she reached down into the deepest registers of her cello, then climbed back up to the higher notes, for some in her audience could hear only the deep notes, and some could hear only the high bright melodies. She played the quiet passages *forte*, so that everyone could hear them, and filled the room with passion and vitality. She had almost everyone in the audience with her now, staring at her while her bow swept back and forth and her fingers worked the four strings. Those few who did not seem to register that she was playing—a man who slumped to one side in his chair and dozed, a woman who rocked back and forth as she stared straight ahead—may still have heard a portion of what she was playing. Astrid wanted to fill them with the joy that had once come from life itself, and now must come from the heart of a cello.

She played mountain songs for these mountain people. Several of her listeners had at one time, like herself, lived in a cabin built of logs. They liked to hear the songs they had once danced to, liked to hear the ballads they had hummed while they hiked over a misty mountain pass. Magnus too, of course, liked to hear those old mountain songs. He watched her while she played, his blue eyes full of love, and not some remembered love.

Then there was a short intermission, while the nurses made a quick check around the room, but not a single member of the audience departed. Magnus stood ready to push the button on a tape recorder, which would play through two speakers just behind her chair, one on each side. The second half of the program would be the classical portion of the concert, for many in the audience loved to hear their Grieg, or Mozart, or Beethoven. Astrid often played a selection from what she would be playing at the Concert House that evening, and so she did now. She nodded, Magnus pushed the button, then he quickly crossed the room and sat beside Mama. Mama raised her hand so he could put his hand on her armrest, then she placed her hand back on his.

Astrid began as the lone voice in the orchestra, for Rossini's "William Tell Overture" opened with a solo for the first cello, grieving with deep sadness. She played over the lone cello on the tape, masking it completely.

Now the other cellos came in, though not yet either violin or bass; her sister cellos echoed her plaintive grief. In the eleventh bar, the bass entered, first *legato*, then *pizzicato*, plucking quietly beneath her song, *dolce*. The timpani gave a growl. Her sad, gentle song remembered a beautiful time long ago; in measure thirty-six, she climbed up to a sustained trill, a quiver of longing, and the timpani growled again. With resignation, the cellos quieted to *pianissimo*; then Astrid climbed one final time to a high clear A, with a touch of vibrato, and now up a full octave to her highest A, sustained.

The nervous violins and violas began their *allegro* frenzy. A piccolo peeped. Astrid could see in Mama's eyes that Mama already recognized the piece.

The tension grew steadily: the woodwinds chirped their worry and warning, the strings trembled, the timpani faintly rumbled. The horns entered, the *crescendo* steadily built, and then . . .

Rossini's storm was a mountain storm; it struck with savage fury. Two of the men in the audience smiled with delight, although one woman with a white lace collar over her eggplant-blue velvet dress grimaced with fright, as sheets of rain blasted the landscape, the wind shrieked overhead, and timpani thunder roared. The volume of the recorded music was not loud; Astrid's listeners were delicate. But it was loud enough that she could really dig her bow into the strings while the horns rose to the fore, cymbals clashed, and the bass drum thumped. The audience weathered the storm, for not a single person left the room.

Then Lillian's flute came to calm them, Anne Cecilie's English horn to soothe them. While the alto oboe piped with a steady gracefulness, and a triangle chimed, the flute became a jubilant nightingale, its call a dancing silver pearl of sound, lilting joyously in a distant wood. Astrid saw smiles blossom in the audience, six, seven, eight of them.

And now of course came Per Olaf leading the charge with his galloping trumpet! A half-dozen wheelchairs immediately became steeds. Magnus, as ever, grinned with pure exuberance. Astrid loved taking this roomful of people for such a ride. The trumpets awakened every soul, the driving strings encouraged every heart. She bowed with all her might to keep up with the orchestra, every instrument galloping, galloping.

A final defiant blare from the horns, and now the triumphant drumrolling E from all the orchestra. It was a magnificent, rousing finale . . . followed by silence in the room, and then a scattered but vigorous clapping of elderly hands.

Ha! She had done it, full blast and never missed a measure. She was ready, with full confidence, for tonight.

She saw the pride in her mother's eyes, pride and love—and a treasure of fresh memories of music—that would carry her through the week. A long week, like a steep rocky mountain slope, gray and lonely. Mama would walk her path until one last slope, reaching toward a misty mountain pass, took her to the sleep of eternity.

Astrid, with her cello named *Birkebeiner*, would be with her mother along every step of that final journey.

CHAPTER 12

Wearing a pink T-shirt and khaki shorts, Eli Margrethe walked with her violin in its black leather case down Majorstuveien (which became Uranienborgveien) to the northern corner of the Palace Park. While she crossed the broad rolling sweep of brown grass and bare trees, she saw that many people were out, walking, jogging, sunbathing topless, riding bicycles and laughing. The first day of spring had thrown open the doors of Oslo; here and there among the thick dark tree trunks, people with very white legs simply stood and lifted their faces to the brilliant sun.

As she walked through the park, she pushed up the sleeves of her pink T-shirt so that her shoulders were bare, trading the violin case from hand to hand as she did so. She looked up at the branches above her, saw the faint reddish swelling of buds at the ends of the twigs. The clearest blue sky she had seen in months arched over the park, over the stately yellow Palace. As she neared the spot where she would play today—a small rise above a pond, with the tall yellow and white wall of the Palace just behind her—she was pleased. She had her outdoor theater, she had her peripatetic audience, and now she would play some old songs from the sea. She would work on the vocal section of the second movement. On her violin, she would experiment, transforming the simple melodies of the songs into something orchestral, something symphonic. She needed five or six songs, in the right sequence, flowing from one to the next, with the cello playing quietly but steadily in the background: the great wave that never stopped rolling.

When she reached the top of a small grassy slope overlooking the little pond, she stepped off the gravel path, set the black case down in the grass and opened its latches. She took out her violin, which, today, felt more like a blessing than a curse. She felt ready to play those old songs that her grandfather had sung for her with his rumbling salty voice.

And if she played a love song, she could imagine a lad up north, out on his boat under this same blue sky, tanning his cheeks with this same bright sun, and wondering if ever he would meet the woman whom his heart was aching to find. Yes, she could play well today; she could feel it in her, as an athlete could feel that she was ready to run.

Eli Margrethe lifted the violin to her shoulder and admired the three-hundred-year-old masterpiece, dark brown with a tinge of red in the sunshine. She raised her bow to the blue sky, in a salute to the Creator who had blessed her. Then with a sweep of horsehair, she gave the world a clear, bright, high C-sharp, exactly on key from the first attack. She sustained the note, with a bit of *vibrato*; people walking across the park turned their faces toward the unusual sound. She fingered down the octave to middle C-sharp. Then she scampered back up again, in C-sharp minor, pouncing on the high C-sharp. She soared up another octave, dusting the attic with an *arpeggio*, so that she had fully awakened the soul inside her instrument.

While baby buggies passed on the gravel path behind her, she played all the old songs she had learned as a girl from her grandfather. Whenever he wasn't working and the weather was good, he had taken her out on his fishing boat from the Henningsvær harbor to the open sea, just the two of them, their special time together. As they sang song after song, her child's voice and his walrus voice blended with the chug-chugging of the boat's engine.

Ripples on the little pond, stirred by a breeze through the park, sparkled in the sunshine. She played the slow sad song of a fisherman who misses his sweetheart. It was a song to be sung over the gunnel of a boat, a song to be sent across the cold gray sea, while a man's half-frozen hands were working the heavy lines. His words, while he sang, became a mist that quickly disappeared in the frigid air.

She played a song about homesickness, worse almost than loneliness, for a woman warms a man's heart, but his country is the bedrock beneath his feet.

She played songs about the codfish, could have played a dozen songs about the cod. She played a song about Russian cod becoming Norwegian cod, as immense schools of codfish swam against the Gulf Stream toward the Lofoten spawning waters. The eggs and young fish then drifted north and east on the oceanic river to the nearly frozen sea above Russia. She realized that she needed a Russian song about the sea, and wondered where she might find one.

Her violin sang of wooden boats with burly men at the oars, and of heavy canvas sails that rumbled in the wind. Her violin sang about tired men who slept in wooden huts on the rocky shore. Each hut had at least one square hole cut into its log wall: the window was covered with the dry skin of a halibut's belly.

Her violin sang of the coastal steamer that rang its bell at every port. Her music conjured the bustling wharves, the lonesome piers, and people trundling with their bundles up the gangplank while the ship's brass railing shone with a golden glow in the midnight sun.

Eli Margrethe was playing an ancient hymn that people sang while their men were at sea . . . when she heard a unique and intriguing voice. A man was singing in some strange manner; he was calling out sounds that may or may not have been words, in a long flow of notes that were not quite a melody. She recognized the singing as Sami; looking beyond one end of the pond, she spotted the singer himself. He had just entered the park from Parkveien, and now turned left onto a path that would take him along the other side of the pond. He was looking at her, for she was still playing her Christian hymn.

She played to the end of the verse, then she lifted her bow and listened to him sing. He strode along the path as if he were setting out to cross fifty kilometers of tundra today. He turned his face toward her: his singing bounced and rolled as if it too were crossing some vast terrain.

Then he surprised her, because he stopped singing and stood facing her, the pond between them.

He pointed up through the bare branches at the sun. "Bah-EEE-vash bah-EEE-tah," he called to her. Then he called in English, "The sun is shining!"

He spoke slowly, clearly, offering to teach her the words. She accepted the offer. "Bah-EEE-vash bah-EEE-tah," she called back to him. She pointed her bow at the sun shining over the Palace, then she laughed as she too called in English, "The sun is shining!"

"Bueh-reh," he called. "Good!"

Then he was walking again, singing again, past the far right corner of the pond, his voice no doubt reaching out to the northern half of the park. People turned to listen; they heard as well a violin that tried to replicate the bouncing melody, the strange yet confident tones.

Eli Margrethe decided that as she would need a Russian song, so she would need a Sami *yoik* in the vocal portion of the second movement, for the Samis had fished along the coast for thousands of years.

And then of course, to make it all symphonic.

It was good that no one but Astrid knew that she was writing a symphony. Because the more she thought and wrote and listened, the more she understood how immense a job it was that she had tackled. To write a symphony was to draw the complex blueprint of a cathedral. Towering, intricate, monumentally beautiful, both symphony and cathedral required a willingness to struggle for years.

She thought about Tchaikovsky: no one had ever understood happiness better than that poor lonely man. He gave the world so much joy, then he wrote his last symphony as if he already lay in his grave.

She lifted her bow, lowered her violin, and listened carefully, but could no longer hear the Sami's voice.

If it took five years to write a symphony, it took five years. What could a person do with such a blessing and a curse?

CHAPTER 13

Lillian stood up from the campfire, a cup of coffee in one hand, her flute in the other. She walked in her boots across the grassy earth (still sodden from melted snow), stepped onto the long wooden pier, then walked out toward its end: she was soon surrounded by the huge gray oval of ice. Peering down, she saw that the ice had begun to melt around the pilings. At the end of the pier, she sipped her coffee and, awake now, prepared to bid the world good morning.

Bjørn walked behind her with his cup of coffee; his two conga drums were already out on the pier. He had taken his shirt off in the morning sunshine, and wore just his jeans and hiking boots. Lillian wore jeans and boots, and a pink spaghetti-strap blouse, her white shoulders lovely.

Lillian had to squint when she glanced south across the ice. But looking north, she could rest her eyes on the dark green forest along the edge of the frozen lake. She savored her coffee, savored the hills that invited her eyes to wander. Then she set her cup down on the worn gray wood of the pier, raised her flute to her lips, and let Grieg bid the finest good morning of all.

She played the flute part which opened that gladdening song, then she played the oboe's part, and the strings', and the horns', coming back again and again to the flute weaving through the music. She sent her silver notes out over the ice, and bid good morning not simply to the day, but to the First Day of Spring. Today, the buds in the birches would awaken. The spruce would perfume the wind. The waters of the lake would stir. And she was, perhaps, for the first morning in her life, with child.

She breathed in the cool air over the lake, then breathed it out as music. Her Grieg began with wonder and joy, and ended with deep gratitude. She lowered her flute, and heard, from the forest across the lake, the clear twittering chirp of a winter finch.

Bjørn's hands began to tap on the leather heads of his congas, while he gazed across the lake at white birch trunks where the sap was beginning to flow. His hands lightly pattered, for he did not want to disturb, quite yet, the quiet that lay upon the frozen lake.

He remembered when they had first come to this pier, in July twelve years ago. He dove into the warm lake, then swam, as she said, "like an otter." When he bobbed up from underwater at the end of the pier, she was sitting in her coral-orange bikini with her feet over the edge, her toes in the water, the hot afternoon sun full on her face, her blond hair still not wet. She was looking down at him with such delight, that he laughed and asked her, "Won't you come in?" Meaning, without asking her yet, "How deep underwater have you ever kissed a man?"

By the end of the afternoon, he knew: about five meters deep, where in the cool water their warm lips pressed together while he held her shoulders and she held his just about everything.

Lifting her flute once again to her lips—her jazz flute now—she began to play along with Bjørn's drumming just behind her.

She remembered her first trip to Sotra that August a dozen years ago, when he taught her how to paddle a sea kayak. They paddled together from the Telavåg harbor out to a small island off the coast: a bit of smooth grey rock with a tiny beach. The sky was deep blue, summertime blue, not springtime blue like today. The sea was calm, the breeze barely enough to sweep away the heat from the blazing sun. The little slope of sand, cupped in a horseshoe of sea-worn rock, faced the sea (not the island of Sotra), so that all she could see as she sat on Bjørn's towel was the blue of the heavens and the blue of the deep. An occasional white gull sailed over, peering down at their nakedness.

On that tiny island, beside the wash of the sea, in the sweat of the August sun, they made love for the first time. He had been such a gentleman—she nearly died of aching for him—for he had waited until they could be together in Paradise.

* * *

Bjørn's hands began to beat in earnest. He recognized Lillian's song about the sea, about the tiny island in the skerries, about the first time they made love. He remembered holding her hips afterwards, while she lay in a state of collapse on top of him. Maybe in half an hour, they would find the energy to stand up from the beach where they baked in the sun, and wade into the cold water, to wash themselves fresh and clean.

But for now, they would lie in each other's sweat, as if the two of them had melted together.

His hands now slapped a vibrant Cuban flourish, which settled into a bold rhythm, as he remembered what he had suddenly understood when Lillian lifted her head and kissed his sweaty shoulder.

He understood, with absolute conviction, that life had to have a purpose.

The sea did not need them. The little beach in a cleft of rock did not need them. The enormous blue sky did not need them. The sun certainly did not need them. Yet here they were, woman and man, sentient, able to smile, laugh, and touch, able to move beyond friendship into love. And if such creatures existed, as she and he did, in all their beauty and complexity, then there must be some force of life, as real as the force of gravity.

A force with a purpose.

No beauty was given to this earth without a purpose. Lillian wrapped him in beauty.

No love was given to this earth without a purpose. Bjørn's heart beat with a rising tide of love, for Lillian, for the beach and the sea and the benevolent blue sky.

The sun in its blue firmament blessed them in the abundance of their love.

His Lillian. Forever his Lillian. That was the daily miracle. And now while she played her flute, sending her love song up to the sun (her eyes closed, her uplifted face serene), he played his drums as a prayer to the force of life that had granted him these twelve years on earth with a woman of such beauty. And purpose. And faith.

Part III

Silver Ribbons

CHAPTER 14

Inger got her men immediately to work. "Keep an eye out for a couple of spars to the northwest," she told them. "That's our cut to Vestfjorden."

Her crew, seated on the port bench in the cockpit—balancing the wind in the sails—sat up straight, turned their shoulders and stared beyond the oaken bow, each man with a sharp eye for a pair of spars.

"Should I go up on the bow," asked Voldemar, "to watch for shallows? I see waves breaking over those shoals." He pointed west at a distant patch of white, where the rolling waves turned from blue to ruffled foam.

"Yes," she said, "you can keep a watch from the bow."

Voldemar stepped quickly up the three stairs from the cockpit to the port gunnel, then walked gracefully forward along the narrow uplifted deck—he raised his right hand and patted the wooden mast, as if with affection, as he walked past it—to the bow, where he stood with his feet spread wide. With the white jib to his right, and the rushing blue sea to his left, Voldemar swept his eyes over the water to the northwest, looking to spot the spars.

Inger had already spotted them, of course, for in the midday sunshine, they were readily visible—tiny dark stripes bobbing right in the middle of the fjord—if you knew where to look for them. The fjord was over a kilometer wide here, and the two spars could quickly disappear in bad weather. That was why, of course, most of the traffic up the fjord followed Drøbak Sound: to avoid the shoals at the foot of Vestfjorden. But Inger wanted to put her crew to work.

Voldemar spotted the spars when they were still three hundred meters away. He pointed his arm like an arrow straight ahead, then he called back to her, grinning, "There they are!" He knew, of course, by the fact that she was sailing directly toward them, that she had spotted the spars long ago.

Johannes stared from his seat, then he stood up and stared from the forward corner of the cockpit, his feet to the left of the companionway down to the galley, his hands on the edge of the waist-high deck, his eyes staring at the expanse of water beyond the bow. Finally he called out in triumph, "There they are!" He pointed his arm like an arrow straight ahead. Then he turned around and grinned at Inger, his eyes filled with delight. "Dead ahead, they are!"

"Thank you, lads," she told them.

When the red spar to port and the green spar to starboard swept safely past--the tall spars leaned with each wave rolling up from the south—the *Kristine Marie* entered the left fork of the fjord, Vestfjorden, a long channel that bent like a sock from northwest to north, between Håøya Island and the mainland. Rather than simply run with the wind up Vestfjorden, Inger put her vessel and crew through a series of basic maneuvers. She tacked a dozen times, each tack a bit further north, so that her craft slowly zigzagged up the channel. At the end of every tack, she came about, swinging her prow to the south and across the strong wind. Her crew thus repeated the drill a dozen times.

Standing at the oaken wheel in the rear of the cockpit, she called out the sail changes; Voldemar called back in his English with an Estonian accent that he understood, then he showed Johannes exactly what to do. Though Johannes was very unsteady on his feet the first time he climbed the steps and walked forward to the bow, he learned quickly. Following Voldemar's instructions, Johannes moved awkwardly from position to position on the vessel, then paid close attention to each step of his job with the lines and sails.

Inger steered slowly into each coming-about, carving a grand curve into the wind. Again and again, she brought Papa's bow due south and felt the wind fresh on her face; again and again, Voldemar and Johannes handled the jib sheets with increasing skill. Inger sailed in big waltzing curves, as if Vestfjorden, a broad quiet stretch of water away from commercial traffic, had become her ballroom.

When the *Kristine Marie* had passed the northern end of Håøya Island, Inger was able to sail toward the middle of the fjord, where she could then sail due north. She no longer zigzagged, but ran with the wind off her starboard quarter. Her two men stood on the bow, their feet spread wide on the tilted deck, watching the other sailboats and waiting for further orders. Voldemar looked peaceful and alert. Johannes looked ready for whatever was next.

For a few minutes, she let herself relax. The *Kristine Marie* was sailing beautifully; the wind was steady; and her crew could handle the lines. The sun shone warmly on her back. And her eyes could reach far up the fjord. The water today was a magnificent blue, beneath a crystalline blue sky.

She loved to feel the boat rolling beneath her feet, loved to grip the spokes of the wheel. She was almost as free as the three gulls that swooped and whirled above her, their long white wings so crisp against the pure blue.

Voldemar saw that Inger was clearly a most competent captain. The sails had been properly stowed, the little galley was neat, and she was very exact about the coiling of her lines. She trimmed her sails well, liked a tight jib. And she certainly taught her pupil Johannes how to work the sheets.

It all gave Voldemar hope for the concert tonight.

Johannes liked the simplicity and order and common sense of the sailboat. He learned how to cleat and uncleat a line. How to pull, or release, the jib sheet, while the big triangular sail flapped across the deck and then puffed out on the other side. Though neither he nor Voldemar knew all the correct nautical terms in English, they managed to make themselves clear to each other. Working together through each change in the sailboat's direction, student and master kept the jib in good trim.

Once, when Johannes noticed that Inger was watching him, he gave her a smile of gratitude. She had picked him up out of a coffin, had brought him back to the world of the living.

He wondered if she had ever visited Tchaikovsky's home in Klin. He himself had visited Moscow many times, and of course St. Petersburg, but he had never had the time to take a train north from Moscow to Klin. He would like to spend an entire day first visiting the house, then walking the grounds where Tchaikovsky had walked.

Tchaikovsky's piano still stood in the main room on the second floor (as he had read in a guidebook). Outside the window of Tchaikovsky's small office stood a cluster of white birches, the same birches which the composer had looked at while he sat at a birch table and wrote his last symphony.

Johannes wondered if, after the season's final concert in May, Inger would like to visit Tchaikovsky's home in Russia.

Once the captain had reached a point from which she could sail due north up the broad belly of the fjord, she brought her stern closer and closer to the wind while Voldemar let the mainsail swing further out to port. The jib, caught from behind, flapped restlessly. Voldemar and Johannes each took a sheet and brought the jib across to starboard. Voldemar showed Johannes how to let the jib swing out until the two sails, mainsail and jib, port and starboard, wing and wing, roughly balanced each other. Now the wings could do their work, and the musicians could turn their attention to Beethoven.

"Thank you, lads," Inger called to them. "You can get out the score now and go to work."

Her two sailors walked back along the starboard gunnel (thus balancing the bigger sail) to the cockpit. Both gave a nod to the captain at the wheel, then both went down the steps to their quarters below, Johannes to get his glasses, Voldemar to fetch his score. When, a minute later, they both came back up the steps, each of them glanced at Inger at the wheel and gave her a grin. The sun shone full upon their faces in that moment, caught the color in Voldemar's dark amber eyes, and quickened the color in Johannes's blue eyes.

They sat on the starboard bench in the cockpit, a bench of varnished maple, shoulder to shoulder with the score on Voldemar's lap. Voldemar opened the black cover to the score's first page, then he pointed to the first measure, at which Johannes peered closely.

Inger, watching them from the wheel, now said, "Voldemar, as you know, the very first note in Beethoven's Fifth Piano Concerto is *tutti*: the entire orchestra plays a powerful E-flat chord, while the piano is silent. Only after the first four beats do you come in with your opening cadenza. The piano does not begin the concerto with the orchestra. It is born out of the orchestra's opening chord."

She said nothing further. She would let Voldemar interpret that observation as he wished.

Johannes, being a conductor, could sing the orchestra's part. Voldemar, being a pianist, could sing the piano's part. Not every note, of course, but certainly the general flow, the phrasing, the *crescendo* and *decrescendo*, the wavering trills, and the attacks. Thus Johannes sang the opening E-flat (below middle C) for four beats, then Voldemar sprang to life with a magnificent run of notes.

Piano and orchestra played the second *tutti* together. Then the piano ran off on its own again, with increasing confidence.

Piano and orchestra played the third *tutti* together. The piano, "Solo (Vivace)", took off on its third run, which diminished into a trill, and moved quietly with a silver sprinkling of notes to a final, brief, one-chord *tutti* with the orchestra.

Whereupon the piano, as if going back to sleep, relinquished the next several minutes of music solely to the orchestra.

Voldemar, however, did *not* relinquish to Johannes the tempo of the orchestral passage. While Johannes sang the part, Voldemar counted the beat with his hand, as would a conductor with his baton. Inger could see immediately that Voldemar had received some training as a conductor, for he was not only accurate in counting the beats, but also very sure of himself. Johannes, a well-trained singer in his youth, followed his conductor's beat exactly as he sang the long solo passage.

Finally, well into the concerto, piano and orchestra played together. Steady at the wheel, Inger enjoyed the two male voices running through their parts in perfect tandem. Though Voldemar was still turning the pages of the sunlit score on his lap, neither man needed to see what was written on it. Inger heard a love for the music in Johannes's voice, a love which had not been present in any of the earlier rehearsals.

Johannes was becoming himself again; he seemed to discover stores of energy as he sang. He never corrected Voldemar's tempo: as in days of old, Voldemar conducted from the keyboard. Johannes's job was to keep the members of the orchestra in step with the piano, which, Inger knew, they had been aching to do all week.

Inger could have sung the violin part, but she did not want to interfere with their rehearsal. She kept her eye on her sails, on her compass, on her telltales, on the other sailboats running and beating around her. Far ahead was the port of Oslo, of Kristiania: the same port toward which people had been sailing on a day like today, five thousand years ago.

She slipped off her sneakers so she could stand barefoot on the warm oaken deck.

CHAPTER 15

Murphy dug a hole among the apple trees while Per Olaf turned the soil of the fenced-in garden. Per Olaf wanted to play a fanfare early this evening, at around six o'clock. Two hours, at least, before the concert at eight. Inger would give him a signal—if and when she arrived on time in the Oslo Harbor with Johannes—whether it was thumbs up, or thumbs down. If he spotted her red sail, he would race to the restaurant to let the orchestra know that the concert was on.

Murphy wasn't worried about any of that. He wanted to smell like black earth nurtured with years of rotten apples.

Per Olaf stepped on the blade of his shovel, felt the curved steel slip into the firm soil, then he took hold of the handle and turned over another lump of rich black earth. He would outline first the vegetable garden with a rectangle of turned earth, and then the smaller flower garden. He had been outlining the two gardens since he was a kid, doing it for his mother. She liked a sharp edge along her garden, not a ragged edge made by the plow. (Later today, Odd would turn the soil of both gardens with the Turbotiller, an old monster that roared and puffed its oily fumes.) Every spring, Per Olaf outlined the family gardens. And though the work did grow a bit tiresome toward the end, clod after clod after clod, it gave him time to think.

"You're a darn fool," he told himself.

"Why is that?" he asked.

"Because you've been thinking about this for five years, and you ain't done a darn thing yet."

"Yes, but it's an undertaking, you know. Expense, and paper-work, and consent from the neighbors. Then we put it up, and what? Does it work? Does it pay for itself? Or does it make me look like a darn fool?"

So it was that Per Olaf considered the matter. He wanted to do it, wanted to leave behind something more than a tombstone. He would be sixty in September, and he wanted to give himself, and the neighborhood, a birthday present. He wanted to erect a monument, not to himself, but to the wind and the sun and the earth. He was a born farmer, and saw things from a farmer's point of view. He loved the land, loved to turn it with a shovel, loved to plow it with the tractor, loved to walk it in every season. He wanted to give something back to the land. More than just another body in a grave.

As he turned the good black earth along the edge of the ragged brown garden, he realized that though it was a nice notion to put the wind turbine out in the pasture, they would have to spend a lot of money on a long cable to carry the electrical power. A kilometer of cable, at least. So why not put the turbine in that unused plot of grass behind the barn? Nothing there now but the old log barn, the first barn built on the farm, and a patch of grass that kept six goats happy all summer. Stand the wind turbine behind the barn: a turbine with a white tubular tower four times higher than the barn roof. And four times the height of the chestnut trees behind the little goat pasture. Put up a giant tubular stem, then let three giant white daisy petals catch the wind.

Ja, thought Per Olaf, it would be nice to know every morning at dawn that the breeze off the fjord was heating his first cup of strong coffee.

And the old barn . . . the logs were rotten now around the base. Why not clear it away, then build a school on the site: a small log building, one room, with a lot of windows, and about twenty desks. He would continue to gather books and journals for a library on wind turbines, and he would put a map up on the wall, showing where in the world turbines could be found. (Every red pin would represent another ten.) It would be a school open to anyone who wanted to learn about wind speeds, wing shape, torque, and clean electricity; a school in session one evening a week when Per Olaf was not at rehearsals. He could invite a class of engineering students from the Agricultural College in Ås. Invite them out to the farm, give them a good practical seminar on How Well Does This Darn Thing Work?

Ja, thought Per Olaf. He would like that, a turbine and a school, for his sixtieth birthday.

Then he got to thinking, as he edged the vegetable garden's first corner, about Voldemar, whose family wanted a wind turbine on their farm so they could be independent from everybody else's oil.

So they could live in peace.

"You know, Per," he said to himself, "you spend all this time thinking about whether or not to put up one lone turbine for your family and your neighbors, when you *should* be thinking about how to help other folks put them up all over the world. In Estonia, for starters."

Because farmland was farmland, and earth was earth. Be it in Norway, Estonia, or deep on the steppes of Russia. Or over where his grandfather's uncle had emigrated to, somewhere in western Minnesota. The wind blesses all land. The sun blesses all land. Seeing things from a farmer's point of view, Per Olaf wondered why it took so long for people to put the wind and the sun to work.

"Well, it took you five years, you darn fool."

Per Olaf began to think, while he was digging, that he would like to play a fanfare, right now. He wanted to let old Torstein and Hulda know that the farm was about to take a major step forward.

So he shoved the steel blade into the firm earth, then left his shovel where it stood. As he walked toward the garden gate, he took off his old gloves; nine out of ten fingers were poking through the frayed ends. He looked over at Murphy in the apple orchard, on the other side of the fence. The dog was shoulder deep, his black rump in the air, his head almost hidden. "Murph, I'll be right back."

The dog lifted his black and filthy head and looked at Per Olaf briefly; then he returned to his digging.

Per Olaf crossed the yard and stepped up to the porch, then he sat on an old kitchen chair and took off his rubber boots. (The chair had a loose back, but its four maple legs were still good.) Leaving his boots outside, he stepped in his socks into the farmhouse. He glanced around the empty kitchen—where the family had gathered that morning to listen to Voldemar speak on the phone with Johannes—then he climbed the stairs to his office. He did not fetch the trumpet which he would play tonight in the Concert House, God willing. Instead, he took down from its felt-padded rack on the wall a long straight Fourteenth Century British horn, a horn made for royal tuckets and flourishes and fanfares. He carried the ancient horn—it was two meters, eight centimeters long from its mouthpiece to its flaring bell—carefully down the stairs, around the banister at the bottom, along the hallway, then through the kitchen to the kitchen door, which he had left open. Outside on the porch, he stepped into his rubber boots. Then he walked with his Plantagenet horn down the porch steps into the midday sunshine. He paused to gaze with loving eyes at his trumpet's gleaming brass.

As he walked with long strides past the partly-edged garden, he called, "Murphy!" The dog came bounding out of the apple orchard. When Murphy ran past Per Olaf, with dirt and leaves and a bit of brown fern tangled in his fur, Per Olaf wondered to which kingdom Murphy belonged: animal or plant?

Per Olaf set out along the ridge, following exactly his footsteps at dawn with Voldemar. His eyes wandered over the rolling brown hills. He felt the sun strong on his face. The seeds in the earth were awakening today. Buds were awakening. Frogs deep in the mud at the bottom of the pond (the ice had disappeared a few days ago) were awakening. A gust of wind buffeted his face, wind that smelled of awakening pines.

After walking along the broadening crest of the ridge for a kilometer, he reached the burial mound. Turning around, he looked back at the tall red barn flanked by two white farmhouses. He imagined a straight white stem towering behind the barn, with three long slender white petals spinning slowly in the blue sky. Spinning with slow graceful dignity.

It would take some getting used to, this giant thing on their land. But Anne Cecilie and Ingeborg and Odd were all for it. Had been for two years.

Per Olaf raised the long golden horn to his lips and played "A Fanfare for Saint Olaf," which he himself had written as a boy. He had played it every spring for forty-eight years. Each four-bar phrase was a declaration of regal pomp and dignity. Sending his bold brassy notes across the land, he did not announce, but *proclaimed*, The First Day of Spring.

Turning slowly where he stood, so that the long gleaming horn moved like an arm of a clock, Per Olaf played his fanfare again and again for the awakening seeds in the rolling brown earth; for the buds in a distant grove of gray maples; for the frogs in the pond at the foot of the gully where the cattle watered.

When he had turned in a half-circle from north all the way to south, he closed his eyes and lifted his face to the warm sun, then he played his fanfare *vivace* for the king of this earthly kingdom. He played as well for the wind, a river of energy, sweeping across the land. He took breath after breath of that wind, then sent it out his trumpet's brass bell as music which the wind would carry as it swept another kilometer and turned three imaginary white blades.

Pointing his horn toward eight o'clock (if north were twelve and south were six), he played for Torstein and Hulda inside their mound of stones. He let his ancestors know that the land would *not* be lost to a century of artificial warming. The crops would not wither as the sun scorched the earth. The creeks would not become silent, and the pond would not become a round black crust. With intelligence and turbines around the world, there would always be, for the next thousand years, another First Day of Spring.

Now he pointed his horn toward ten o'clock, toward (hidden beyond the fringe of the spruce forest) the upper reach of the fjord. He played his jubilant fanfare for the rolling blue water, and for the sloop sailing north toward the Concert House.

He wished the captain and crew a most successful voyage.

CHAPTER 16

Inger had her eye on the Asker skerries to the northwest, while Voldemar and Johannes proceeded *con bravura* toward the finale of the first movement.

After a brief pause at the end of the first movement, the orchestra and then piano began the second movement, the "Adagio." The two men sang with such tenderness that Inger took her eyes from the fjord for half a minute to watch them. Johannes sang with gentle power. Voldemar sang with extraordinary delicacy, his voice just audible, but extremely clear. Staring out at the fjord, Voldemar conducted the tempo with his slowly beating hand.

By the time piano and orchestra attacked the third movement (they crept up to it quietly, then the piano pounced on the "Rondo" with magnificent confidence), Inger could see the small gray nondescript islet in the skerries where her father had always anchored.

She held her course steady, due north, wing and wing, through the concerto's entire third movement. Her men sang with celebration, with triumph. When a schooner fetching tight to the wind passed the *Kristine Marie* about fifty meters to port, its captain and crew turned their faces toward the duet booming Beethoven over the water.

Following the piano's final exuberant run, and the orchestra's Beethovenian march toward an irrevocable resolution, the final E-flat chord, . . . the two men were silent. Inger watched them. Voldemar held out his hand to Johannes (the hand with which he had been beating time); Johannes took Voldemar's hand and the two men shook with mutual congratulations. They had done it. And they could do it again tonight in the Concert House.

Inger lifted her hands briefly from the wheel and applauded.

Johannes, emerging from the music, looked around him at two

99

friends, the sailboat, and the sea. For a while, for a long while, he did not think in words, he did not think in music; instead, he simply gazed out at the blue water and savored the first real happiness he had felt for years.

Voldemar knew now, without a doubt, that tonight he would be the voice that his people needed him to be. They would listen as he played, they would listen to the voice that spoke for Estonia. And Anu, wearing her headphones in the studio in Tallinn: she would be listening too. She would hear the music of the man she had always believed in.

Yes, he knew now, without a doubt, that he and Johannes were ready.

"Gentlemen," Inger said to them, "we are going fishing."

She called out the sail changes; Johannes and Voldemar shifted the sails from wing and wing to a broad reach with wind over the port quarter, as the *Kristine Marie* now headed northwest toward her father's favorite fishing hole.

She easily found the spot among the scattered gray granite islets. She brought her bow into the wind, then called to Voldemar, standing on the prow, "Let go the anchor!" He gave the anchor a masterful toss, so that it made a graceful arc with its flanks ready to grab the sandy bottom, then splashed into the shallow blue water. Both sails luffed as the sloop drifted stern-first with the wind. Voldemar let out the anchor line until Inger called, "Enough!" He cleated the line; the sloop came to rest with her bow to the south, and her stern directly over the best codfish hole in all of Oslo Fjord.

The three sailors worked together to drop and secure the sails. Then Inger opened the bow hatch from below, rolled up a thin mattress from one of the bunks, and fed it lengthwise up through the hatch to Voldemar's waiting hands. "Spread it on the deck, please."

She rolled a second mattress and fed it up through the hatch to Johannes's waiting hands. "Spread it on the deck, please."

She gathered her fishing gear from a closet, then climbed the steps from the galley up to the wheel deck with her rod pointed carefully at an upward angle ahead of her. She crossed the cockpit to the transom and peered with keen anticipation into the deep blue water off the stern. Setting down her father's tackle box, she glanced over her shoulder to see how her crew were doing.

They had followed her instructions precisely: Voldemar and Johannes had spread the two mattresses beside each other on the bow, then had lain down with their pillowed heads toward the prow and their feet toward the stern. Both had taken off their shirts in the warm sunshine, and both had rolled up their shirts and laid them over their eyes. Either one or both of them might still have been awake on the gently rolling deck; but after the past few nights, both musicians would soon be sound asleep.

Good, thought Inger. Now I can go fishing in peace.

She put a Swedish jig on her line, a long triangular lure that glinted silver in the water like an injured herring. By early April, the cod would have come up from their winter depths, looking for bristle worms. She held her rod over the stern, then released the jig: it dropped into the sea with a splash that she loved.

She let the jig sink to the bottom, then brought it up a meter so that it hung just above the bottom, as her father had always done. She lifted her rod again and again, working the jig up and down . . . up and down in the cold blue-black water, where the metal would catch the faint glow of the April sun. A glimmer in the depths, just enough for a cod to lunge at.

She wondered, as she stood with the sun warm on her back, the wind tousling her hair, whether Johannes would like to sail down the entire length of the fjord, then cross the Baltic, to Tallinn. They could meet Voldemar at the wharf. He had mentioned that his girlfriend's family had a sloop. What fun to sail together on the Gulf of Finland during the days, and to moor together in the harbor each evening. Two weeks without a telephone. That would be heaven. Johannes could molt right out of his old skin, and get a bit of sun on his new one.

She brought the Swedish jig up a few meters, then lowered and lifted her rod with a varying rhythm. She could feel the heavy lure wobbling when she lifted it.

Johannes had told Martin that he was from Narvik. She had never known that he was from Narvik. How could he have grown up on the coast and be so unfamiliar with a boat?

Lifting her Swedish jig again and again, she remembered the time that her mother and her father both caught a fish at the same moment. While they were reeling in, one cod swam around the other and got the lines tangled. Mama thought at first that a whale had grabbed her codfish! They had to stand shoulder to shoulder at the stern, Mama and Papa, and reel in together. The lines became so badly wound around each other that Papa set down his rod and reached over the transom to grab hold of the two lines together; he pulled them up hand over hand. When he had brought the thrashing cod to the surface, he called out, "Coming aboard!" Then he hauled the two beautiful yellow-brown codfish over the transom. They flopped on the deck, both as long as Papa's arm. Mama laughed and asked, "Which one is mine?"

They were always so happy out on the boat, her parents. The *Kristine Marie* was their escape from the restaurant in Drøbak, where Papa worked as a chef and Mama as a waitress. For forty years. Everyone loved Papa's cooking. But not a single customer in that restaurant ever tasted codfish as good as what Mama boiled up in the *Kristine Marie's* galley.

Her parents had—

She felt the bite: the sudden powerful tug on the line, bowing the tip of her rod nearly to the water. She jerked the rod to set the hook, then she began to reel against the thrashing energy fifteen meters deep. She couldn't feel its weight yet, only its strength. She brought the fish up slowly, enjoying the wild tugs on her rod. This cod was clearly big enough to feed all three of them for lunch. Ho, she was going to provide a *feast* for her men today!

She brought the cod, as long as Papa's arm, up to the surface, where it dashed back and forth on the short line. Then she reached down with the gaff, hooked the big fish in its gill, and hauled her prize over the transom. Safe. (She had lost too many fish at the last moment to call any fish "safe" until she could hear it flapping on the deck.)

She regretted catching lunch so quickly. She would have liked to fish until sunset. Until midnight.

She opened her father's tackle box, took out his knife and slit the cod's throat. Then she held the gleaming yellow-brown fish in her hands and felt how cold it was: as cold as the April sea. When the bearded, gasping cod had stopped quivering, she unhooked the jig from its mouth. She would have liked to show off her catch to her crew, but her crew—one of them was snoring—were off duty now.

She laid a cutting board on the transom, then cleaned her catch. When she tossed a gob of intestines overboard, she heard the shriek of the first gull to arrive. The big white bird grabbed the mass of guts the moment it hit the water.

Inger tossed an old oaken bucket on a line into the sea, then hauled it up arm over arm. She rinsed nine thick slices of white meat in the bucket. Then she put the slices, still cold, into Mama's old green China bowl.

She lowered the bucket a second time, hauled it up and rinsed the blood and slime from the transom.

She hauled up a third bucket of sea water, then carried it down the steps to the galley, where she half-filled two pots on the little stove. She'd boil potatoes long enough in the first pot, then add the codfish to the second pot. It was all in the timing.

While the potatoes simmered, Inger stood at the stove in the slightly stale air belowdecks—air that always smelled of musty bedding and old wood—and remembered her first real voyage on the *Kristine Marie*: a voyage to Copenhagen. She was ten, and so astonishingly talented on the violin in the Drøbak School Orchestra that she was ready for lessons at the College of Music in Oslo. But a student at that level needed a professional violin. Not a student violin, although she was on her third student violin now and it was a very good one.

She was by this time the talk of Drøbak; the town was proud of its prodigy. A professional violin was beyond the means of most families, certainly beyond the means of a chef and waitress. So the town took a collection. Inger's violin teacher made inquiries, then recommended a shop in Copenhagen. This was back in 1971, when a Norwegian had to travel abroad to find an excellent seventeenth-century instrument.

She and her parents could have taken the train and then the ferry to Copenhagen. But Mama and Papa wanted to sail. They wanted to take their ten-year-old daughter on the voyage of a lifetime. They made the crossing in June, after school had ended. Mama and Papa listened carefully to the radio, then set sail when the weather promised to hold steady for a week.

True enough, the sun shone warmly, while the wind blew steady from the west. The stars at night formed an immense canopy over the little boat on the enormous black sea. For hours, day and night, she stood on a wooden box between her father and the wheel, her father's hands wrapped over her little hands on the spokes.

They approached the vast Copenhagen harbor in the light of late afternoon, and finally tied their lines to a crowded pier in the dimness of early evening. They did not sleep below, but up on deck, where the three of them could see the lights of the city, and fall asleep listening to the engines and boat horns of ships arriving in the night.

The next morning, they walked through the streets of the fabled Danish capital to the violin shop, where the owner was expecting them. Herr Thorlund-Pettersen knew from speaking on the phone with Inger's teacher what sort of violin the girl was looking for. And he knew from speaking on the phone with the mayor of Drøbak how much money was available for the instrument. Thus he was able to set out eight violins on a long mahogany table, each instrument on a pad of green felt, along with six different types of bows.

Mama and Papa told Inger that she had all day to try the eight violins. She could have two full days if she needed them. They wanted her to be sure that she found the violin which would last her a lifetime.

Leaning over the galley stove, Inger stuck a long-handled fork into a potato: another ten minutes.

So she spent the entire day in that shop, listening to a violin sing with a certain timbre, then listening to another violin sing with a slightly different timbre. She examined the lacquering, inspected each bridge. By noon, she had selected three perfect violins, each of them worthy of a place in a symphony orchestra. The owner nodded his approval, then said to Papa, "Your daughter has an Italian ear."

Her parents took her to lunch at a nearby restaurant, where Mama and Papa luxuriated as a very polite waiter served them their meals.

Then back to the violin shop, and another three hours of listening to the richness of each string as she played it to the limits of its registers, high and low. She listened to hear where each violin's voice was the strongest, and the weakest.

She knew that many hands had held these violins during their three centuries and more. Hands perhaps more gifted than hers would ever become. But she still had a great amount of growing to do. And thus, when the brass ship's clock in the violin shop chimed four, she knew what her decision would be.

She held in her hands the instrument which would enable her to play the way she *dreamed* she would be able to play, one day. The violin had been made in the village of Cremona, in northern Italy, by a member of the Amati family, in 1678. She would never need another violin, even if some day she managed to play with a real symphony orchestra.

Herr Thorlund-Pettersen made a phone call; the money was cabled from a bank in Drøbak to a bank in Copenhagen. Inger was able to walk out of the shop at a little before six in the evening with her treasure. She carried the violin in its black leather case through the streets of Copenhagen as if she carried her soul in the case.

Insurance had been included in the price; nevertheless, Mama and Papa were anxious about their precious cargo on the sloop that night in the harbor, and during the voyage all the way back to Drøbak. But the weather held steady and they met with no pirates.

The mayor (Papa had alerted him by radio), along with a delegation of contributors, met the returning *Kristine Marie* in the Drøbak harbor. Inger showed those good people her beautiful violin, and played a few notes for them. A week later, when she gave a solo concert in the school auditorium, every seat was filled.

She stuck the long fork into a potato again, felt just the right firmness. She poured the slices of cod from the green bowl into the second pot of boiling water. Then she leaned her face over the pot and took deep breaths of codfish steam.

The violin was now in her locker at the Concert House. Waiting for tonight.

What about the baskets of food from Ingeborg and Anne Cecilie? The bottles of milk from Odd. She and her men would have to drink the milk with lunch, followed by a cup of galley coffee. The picnics could wait until tomorrow. Sunday. Maybe she and Johannes could sleep on two well-aired mattresses tonight, up on the deck where they could see the lights of the city, and fall asleep hearing the engines and boat horns of ships arriving in the night. Tomorrow morning, they could walk, she in her black dress and he in his suit, along Karl Johan Boulevard to the Cathedral, to say a prayer of gratitude. After the service, they would walk back to the harbor, hoist the sails, and go waltzing out on the fjord with their many baskets of picnics.

She poked the fork into the white cod meat: perfect. She turned off both burners. Then she set out three restaurant plates, white with blue trim, on the little galley table. Beside them she put three forks and three knives. From her own basket of provisions, she set out a stick of butter on a wooden plate.

Inger climbed the steps from the galley to the wheel deck, climbed the steps to the starboard gunnel, then walked forward to a spot near the mast where she stood and admired Johannes's bare chest. He had been sweeping that baton for over thirty years, and his muscles showed it.

"Gentlemen, lunch is served."

Voldemar groaned. He lifted the blue shirt from his eyes, then slowly sat up, blinking at the bright sunshine.

Inger had to nudge Johannes's sneaker with her bare foot before he finally stirred. He lifted the brown shirt from his eyes, blinked up at her, then gave her a faint smile. "I think I've been asleep for at least a hundred years."

"Good," she said. "The other nine hundred can come after the concert."

As Voldemar rose to his feet, he asked, "Did you say lunch?"

"Jaah." She said the word good and long, the way her mother used to say it. Then she laughed. "Come see what I have been doing while you two lazy lads have been serving as ballast."

She led her guests down to the galley. Johannes was astonished at the pot of codfish; Voldemar was delighted. With a cod ladle, Inger served big steaming slices of white meat onto the three plates. She gave Voldemar the long fork and let him choose for himself which potatoes he wanted. The young lad chose three big ones.

She sent her men with a plate in one hand and a glass of fresh milk in the other up the steps to the sunshine. They sat, Voldemar on the port bench, Johannes and Inger on the starboard bench, with their plates on their knees. All three of them took deep breaths of the steam from codfish boiled to perfection.

Inger bowed her head and said Mama's favorite prayer.

When she looked up at Voldemar (who had been whispering something in Estonian), she said with a tinge of regret, "We've got only half an hour for lunch. Then we must raise the anchor and be on our way."

He nodded as, with his fork, he separated a piece of meat from the spinal bone. He peeled away the gray skin, pushed the tines of the fork into the steaming white meat, lifted his fork, and bowed his head with gratitude to the fisherwoman. He took the meat into his mouth, then he groaned with heavenly pleasure as he savored his first taste of Inger's codfish.

Johannes stared at her as he too tasted his first chunk of cod. He did not say anything, but she could see a look in his eyes that she had never seen during all the years when he had looked at her from the podium.

CHAPTER 17

Astrid wanted to celebrate her seventieth birthday with her father. She wanted to show him that the cello, which he had sent home in a wagon, had taken her a great distance in life. She wanted to thank him.

She also wanted to show off her students, some from Lillehammer, some from up and down the mountain. She wanted to give her father a small concert, performed by an ensemble of herself and seven gifted, hard-working children. She wanted him to know that such children were still making their way into the world.

Because her father was buried in the southwest corner of the cemetery in the heart of Lillehammer, she wondered if she should phone some village authority, or perhaps the church sexton, for permission to give a concert there. However, after much consideration, she decided that perhaps it was better not to ask.

She *did* ask her seven students if they would be willing to give a concert in a cemetery, a concert for her father who was buried there. The kids were a little surprised at her request, but being kids—from eight to sixteen years old—they readily agreed. Astrid asked them to talk with their parents about the concert. Within two weeks, she had permission from everyone.

So on Saturday, April 5, at a quarter to one in the afternoon, Astrid and Magnus walked the few blocks from their home on Mejdell's Street to the cemetery. Astrid carried a bouquet of twelve red roses; Magnus carried her cello and a folding chair. Along the way, they admired the ancient birches of Lillehammer, rising tall and white into the deep blue sky.

Astrid and Magnus walked down Lange's Street past the high school, then from the upper corner of the park, she spotted her students, clustered near the cemetery gate. When they saw her, they waved. She waved back.

Although heaps of dirty snow still lined Kirke Street, almost all of the snow in the cemetery had melted, revealing last summer's brown grass. The headstones, some black, some gray, stood in widely separated rows. In the middle of the cemetery, the village church warmed its red bricks in the springtime sun.

Astrid and Magnus greeted the seven students at the gate, then Astrid led them along several sidewalks through the cemetery—in a parade of eight cellos in eight black cases, and eight folding chairs— to the southwest corner. As she approached her father's grave, she whispered, "Hello, Papa." She placed the bouquet of red roses on his black headstone.

Following Astrid's instructions, the seven students set their cello cases on the grass, then opened their folding chairs. They arranged the chairs in a semicircle, facing Astrid's father, with Astrid herself in the middle of the arc. The eight musicians sat down, shifted a bit, then nodded to each other that the accommodations were fine.

Then the Great Eight, as they called themselves, stood up again, opened the cases and took out their cellos. The students grinned at each other, for usually they played in the school orchestra, with horns and woodwinds, and the domineering violins. Today they were a gang of cellos.

The musicians sat once again in their arc, bows and cellos ready. Astrid tuned the ensemble, scowling now and then when a student scraped something horrible at her. Soon the four strings on the eight cellos, thirty-two in all, were admirably tuned.

Then there was a pause, a long quiet moment when everyone was ready.

Astrid said, "Shubert's 'Ave Maria.'"

No one needed sheet music. Everyone knew the piece by heart. The students played the reverent music for Astrid's father, and for the hundreds in the cemetery audience around him. They played the piece three times, as a song, as a hymn, and as a prayer.

For her mother in the nursing home, Astrid had played old mountain songs. But for her father, she played classical pieces. He had always been so proud of his daughter during her school concerts. He never stopped marveling that his little girl, born in a log cabin on a mountainside, could step into the world of Schubert, and Mozart, and Beethoven.

While she and her students played through the second piece, a

"Largo" by Händel, she could hear, in the distant background, a speaker at the Lillehammer train station, announcing a train north to Dombås. She and her crew would be on the 15:16 south to Oslo. Every student was coming to the concert tonight. *If* there was a concert. *If* Inger managed to turn Johannes into some semblance of a conductor. Lord help us.

Astrid wanted a seventieth birthday portrait. So Magnus took pictures of his wife with her students from various angles with his old war-horse Nikon. The arc of eight musicians faced Astrid's father, and thus west; the sun was shining from the south. One side of their faces was sharply lit, the other side in shadow. Magnus decided that the best view of the ensemble was Astrid's father's view. So during Wagner's "Sweet Evening Star," he stood on the brown grass behind Øyvind's tombstone. Then he knelt on the sodden earth (for the snow had just melted), focused on Astrid in the deep center of the arc, gave himself as much f-stop as possible, focused again, zoomed back and forth until he placed the ensemble comfortably within the wide-angle frame, and waited.

When Astrid glanced at him with a proud smile, he clicked the shutter.

He liked to watch his wife while she played her cello, liked the intensity and determination of what she did. As a mountain was always a mountain, so Astrid was always Astrid.

And those kids. Eight years old, the one boy, working his fingers as hard as he could. They'd be able to tackle anything, those kids, when their time came. Heart in the right place, and all the confidence in the world.

The ensemble played nine short classical pieces, then concluded the concert with "Lovely is the Earth." Astrid could hear, in the first measures of Norway's sacred anthem, that her students played with a special feeling. They had not only mastered the fingerings and phrasings: they were now able to pour a little of their love into the music.

Reaching deep into the heart of her cello, she poured the fullness of her heart into her father's favorite hymn. She played with gratitude: for sixty years with her precious cello, for sixty-two with Magnus, for seventy years upon this beautiful earth. She played with gratitude and reverence: so that the hymn became a prayer. She prayed that the children beside her would know as beautiful a world as she had known. She prayed that the peacefulness in Lillehammer on this springtime day might spread like a balm over all the world. She prayed that the dead might lie in peace, and that those still unborn might be born in peace.

As she played the final measures, she did not look at Papa's headstone, but at his grassy plot of earth. Beside it was another plot, waiting for her mother. When the day came, Astrid would play old mountain songs at her mother's funeral.

The eight musicians lifted their bows; silence hovered over the cemetery. Astrid turned to the students on her left, then to the students on her right, and told them, "Bravo! Bravo!"

A small crowd had gathered on the sidewalk outside the cemetery. The audience now applauded with hearty gratitude. The Great Eight stood up and bowed.

As her students put their cellos back into the cases, Astrid reminded them to meet her at the train station at 14:45. "Don't be late!"

Then she and Magnus stood, just the two of them, beside her father's grave. "Thank you, Papa," she said. "Thank you for the cello that came up the mountain on a bed of hay in the back of a wagon. Thank you for being a father who saw something special in his little girl."

Magnus, camera in his backpack, cello in his hand, said, "Amen."

CHAPTER 18

A voyage north up Oslo Fjord followed a finger of the sea that reached deep into the land. The *Kristine Marie*, still at anchor, was not quite to the fingertip.

Before Inger left her anchorage in the skerries, she decided that while sailing the last triumphant stretch of the voyage to Oslo, with both conductor and pianist on board in top form, the *Kristine Marie* deserved a red spinnaker.

So she and Voldemar brought up one more sail bag from the locker below. Working together on the bow, they readied the big red sail for hoisting.

Then, while the sloop tugged on its anchor line, they raised the mainsail, and the smaller jib. Both sails flapped as they trailed in the wind.

Back at the wheel, Inger watched Voldemar's bare shoulders as he slowly pulled in and coiled the anchor line. She watched as he lifted the anchor by its chain, hefted the heavy flukes over the lifeline, and placed the anchor by its neat coil of line. (She already knew that without orders, he would later stow the anchor more properly.)

Moving quickly to his next job, he backed the jib: he pulled on the starboard sheet and thus drew the jib at an angle to the wind. The jib then pushed the sloop's bow to the east.

Inger trimmed her mainsail; the sloop picked up speed.

She sailed out of the skerries, then set her course northeast at 55 degrees, toward the northern tip of Nesoddtangen, a large hilly peninsula that jutted into the fjord. She trimmed her two white sails (the spinnaker was still in its bag) to a broad reach with the wind over her starboard quarter. The waves from the south rolled gently under the *Kristine Marie*, lifting the stern and rocking the vessel beneath Inger's feet.

While her hands wrapped around the spokes of the wheel, and her ears listened to the distant cry of gulls, she gazed up at the cerulean sky that arched over the long silver-blue fjord. Today was a blessing. A blessing that no matter what we fools had done during the winter, spring had come back to us once again.

With lunch in their bellies and music in their minds, the three sailors were silent as the sloop cut through the water. They had time and open space enough, finally, to think, to watch, to gaze, to hum a bit, while the wind and the two white wings did all the work.

Then Inger, at the wheel, asked Johannes, standing to her right, "Why didn't you ever say you were from Narvik? In all these years, you've never mentioned the town."

"Ja," said Johannes. Then he paused, one of those long Norwegian pauses which can last a few minutes or a few months. He stared at the sea beyond the bow, his face pinkish-brown from a day in the sun. Then he looked at her as if he were willing to begin a conversation that would last them a lifetime. "I used to go up to visit my mother. But when she passed on, I really had nothing that pulled me back to Narvik."

"What was she like, your mother?"

Johannes stared again at the water beyond the bow. "The only time I've ever been on a boat, before today, was with my mother, on the coastal steamer from Narvik to Bergen." He looked at Inger and admitted, "My father was a seaman who disappeared when I was five. Leaving my mother with three kids to raise. Me the youngest. I can just barely remember my father. My mother received a postcard from him, with a picture of Chicago. No return address. She worked at the fish processing plant in the harbor, heavy work with cold fish eight hours a day. And she had this kid, her third after two daughters, who at the age of twelve could play the piano at school better than anyone had ever played it in the entire history of Narvik. Young Johannes's teacher told his mother that his next teacher would have to be in Bergen or Oslo, and then perhaps Berlin."

Voldemar was listening now, listening to the story of a fellow pianist. He sat on the starboard bench, balancing the sails, watching the sea, and watching as well, with deepening respect, Johannes.

Continuing his boyhood story, Johannes now spoke to both

Inger standing at the wheel on his left, and to Voldemar seated to his right in the cockpit.

"My mother saved every darn penny that she could spare from groceries and school books and clothing for three kids. So that by the time I was fourteen, she could buy two tickets on the coastal steamer to Bergen in May. She bought as well, through the post office, two tickets to a concert, featuring Grieg's 'A-minor Piano Concerto,' in Bergen's Symphony Hall. My mother had the Concerto on an old scratchy record, and we had both heard it a couple of times on the radio. But neither one of us had ever been inside a symphony hall.

"We had a cabin on the steamer with two berths, but aside from sleeping, we were never in it. We were outside on deck during the most beautiful days of May, watching the jagged mountains along Norway's coastline pass slowly by. Watching people busy on the wharf whenever we pulled into a port. Watching the sky turn from deep blue to pale silvery turquoise as day slowly faded into evening, and evening deepened into a springtime night. My mother and I watched the stars rising up over towering black mountains to the east, and watched them sink toward the endless black sea to the west. We never missed a dawn: we savored the golden glow of the sun behind the mountains, before we could see the sun itself.

"My mother had worked almost every week of her life since she was sixteen, and now she was out in the world. She handled it all beautifully. She had already arranged with someone in Narvik who knew someone in Bergen, who took in boarders. So when the steamer docked in Bergen, we walked with our borrowed suitcases down the gangway, felt like world travelers as we walked the streets of the metropolis, passed a little lake in the heart of the city, and found the right street behind the railroad station. My mother knocked on the door. We were warmly welcomed. I think if my mother were here today, she would be running the entire orchestra's travel office."

The three sailors rolled with a particularly large swell; the stern lifted behind them, then they themselves were lifted on the vessel's deck, and now the prow lifted, as if to get a better view of Nesoddtangen far ahead.

"We walked around sunny Bergen that afternoon, and actually had a cup of coffee, Mama and I, in a little café. Then we went back to our room and took a nap. The owner, Fru Bondegaard, promised to wake us at five, in time for a bath and then dinner. The concert was at eight."

Johannes turned to Voldemar. "Do you remember the first time you heard Grieg's 'Piano Concerto,' live in a symphony hall?"

"Of course. My grandfather brought me in from the farm to Tallinn."

"I was fourteen."

"I was eight."

"My mother had bought good tickets. Third row and a little to the left. Maybe my piano teacher had ordered the tickets, I don't know. But the seats were excellent, for we were no more than ten meters from the pianist, and I could clearly see his hands on the keyboard." Johannes paused with a smile of remembrance. "From the first cascade of opening chords, I heard what I had labored so hard to play well, played with magnificence. I watched those two hands with their extraordinary touch, heard phrasings I had never heard before, discovered notes that never before had stood out so clearly. I glanced at my mother: she was totally enraptured. She gripped my hand on the armrest, clearly so proud and happy that she had managed to get me to this concert. She was showing me what it was to be a concert pianist."

Johannes paused again, long enough that Voldemar eventually said, "My grandfather often told my mother that until my first concert, I was only half-born."

"Ja," said Johannes, nodding with agreement.

Then he continued, "After I had listened to the Maestro play some of the softest, saddest elegiac passages I had ever heard, . . . after he had opened up for me a new world of sound in the piano's lower registers, . . . after he had sent chills up my back with the grandeur of his finale, . . . he lifted his fingers from the keyboard. While the applause thundered from the audience, my mother turned in her seat and asked me, 'Is that what you want to do?'"

"'Ja,' I said. 'Ja, I think I can do that.'"

"'All right,' she said, her decision made. 'Then tomorrow we shall make arrangements for you to finish high school here in Bergen. And we'll ask about a piano teacher. Your grandfather left me a little bit that I've never touched. I'm going to sign his bank account over to you.'"

"That's what she said to me. Her hands were always red and raw from handling those cold fish. And she had never been to Oslo even once in her life. But she was going to buy me an education in Bergen."

The three sailed in silence for a while, heard the washing of the waves, heard the distant gulls.

"We spent the night after the concert at the boarding house, then we caught the steamer north the next day." Johannes grinned. "Mama and I discovered that we both had excellent sea stomachs. During a howling storm off the sea, while the big ship pitched and rolled in driving rain, we had the dining room almost to ourselves. After a dessert of ice cream with a small glass of brandy, we stood in our slickers out on the deck in driving rain, watching the storm-shrouded coastline, watching the misty islands, watching the dark rolling sea. My mother stood on the uppermost deck and faced straight into the rain-laden wind, for hours. Before, the sea had been the place where her husband had disappeared, leaving her embarrassed and ashamed. But now during the storm, after the great success of the concert, the sea and the wind and the rain were her own again.

"She would not let me earn any money that summer by working in the fish processing plant. 'You're not going to do that to *your* fingers,' she told me. I was to practice. I would sail once again in August, alone to Bergen.

"During the next few years, my mother came to several student concerts in Bergen. She finally visited Oslo, for my first student concerto—a piece by Mozart—at the College of Music. She was planning to visit me in Helsinki, where I was taking courses in conducting, when her heart quit in the middle of the night and she died at the age of forty-six."

Inger lifted her hand from the wheel and touched Johannes on the shoulder.

"What was your mother's name?"

"Randi. But her friends called her 'Mama Bjørn.' Mother Bear."

"I would like to dedicate our concert tonight to Mama Bjørn. I would like to think that she is looking down, watching her boy on the podium."

"Yes," said Voldemar. "That's right. She and my grandfather can both peer down through the same hole in the clouds."

* * *

Once she had cleared the shallows around Goose Island, off her port, Inger corrected her course to 45 degrees, a heading that would take her past the northern tip of Nesoddtangen, then to the Dyna lighthouse, at the entrance to Oslo Harbor.

She said to her crew, "Why don't you lads hoist the spinnaker?"

Voldemar and Johannes walked forward along the uplifted starboard gunnel—Voldemar gracefully, Johannes a bit less awkwardly—to the bow. Voldemar showed Johannes the spinnaker pole, then the three lines: the brace, the sheet, and the halyard, explaining the purpose of each. Johannes's job was at the halyard: he would pull down on the line and hoist the sail. Voldemar would see to the pole and lines while he made sure the rising sail opened without snagging. Voldemar showed Johannes where to cleat the halyard, once the spinnaker was up. Johannes nodded that he understood.

Voldemar called aft to his captain, "Ready!"

The captain called forward to her crew, "Hoist the spinnaker!"

Inger heard her mother's voice call the words, at a time long ago when Inger and her father had been on the bow.

While Johannes pulled arm over arm on the halyard, and Voldemar guided the clews and luffs and lines and pole, the red sail rose into the blue sky and ballooned with a belly full of wind and sunshine. When the enormous sail was fully hoisted, Johannes cleated the halyard while Voldemar squared and trimmed the clews.

The third sail pulled the sloop at a noticeably greater speed.

Johannes felt, looking up at the huge red sail, that he was inside a big heart, a heart that was pulling the ship. The spinnaker fluttered along its edges, and swung a bit as it pulled.

Voldemar knew, as the red spinnaker pulled him toward the Oslo Concert House, that this evening he would sit down on the black bench and face the keyboard—with the orchestra to his left and the audience to his right—then nod to the conductor that he was ready.

* * *

Inger felt the life in the wheel, in the rudder, in her ship. She kept her eye on her sails, on her compass, on her men. Occasionally she glanced at her watch. They had plenty of time to reach Aker Wharf by six o'clock.

Once the sloop was tied up to a pier, she and her crew would need time below, in shifts, to put on their symphony suits and dress. To comb their hair and look at least a bit civilized. Then all three of them together, dressed in black, would step off the *Kristine Marie* onto the pier and stroll along the wharf. The restaurants would be busy on a Saturday evening, the first warm Saturday of spring. The outdoor tables would be filled with people eating dinner and drinking beer. The three musicians would quietly parade along the wharf, then they would walk up Haakon VII's Street toward the Concert House.

Inger hoped that sometime before six o'clock, Per Olaf would be able to spot the red spinnaker.

CHAPTER 19

Eli Margrethe walked with her violin down the long hill in front of the Royal Palace to the National Theater, then she followed Olav V's Street to the wharf in front of City Hall, where she boarded a ferry for Bygdøy. She had often visited the cluster of museums on the island; she especially enjoyed the models of old fishing boats in the Maritime Museum. But today she wanted to stand in the sea at the edge of the fjord and play her violin. There was a little grassy strip beside the Maritime Museum, a quiet spot away from most of the tourists. Below the strip of grass was a rocky beach. If she took off her sneakers, she could wade into the April-cold water.

She loved riding the ferry; she always stood outside on the open deck. She could finally smell a bit of brine, and her eyes could wander much greater distances over water than they ever could over land. The ferry today was crowded, but she found a spot at the bow railing. The sun shone warmly on her face. She wondered if her cheeks were as pink as her arms were, from playing her violin in the park.

The ferry took her to a pier near the Fram Museum; from there it was a short walk to the strip of last summer's grass. As she set her violin down in its case beside a huge black anchor, she smelled hot dogs. She might even treat herself today, she thought, to an ice cream at the food stand.

She untied her laces, slipped off her sneakers, pulled off her socks. Kneeling on the grass, she opened the case and took out her violin. Then she stepped from the ragged edge of the lawn onto a warm smooth black rock. She stepped down from the rock onto a tiny bit of beach. Then in her pink T-shirt, with the sleeves rolled up over her shoulders, and her khaki shorts, she waded into the cold, gently lapping water. The water was so delightfully cold that it stung her feet. She had to step carefully because of barnacles. She found a sandy spot, where cold little waves washed up to her calves. Facing the fjord, she raised her violin to her shoulder and played a song filled with aching love, the song that her mother still sang to her own father, from the kitchen window while looking out to sea.

The storm took eighteen fishermen from the coast of Norway in one night. Eli Margrethe played the song for her grieving mother, for her lost grandfather, for the eighteen husbands and fathers and sons who never came home.

She waded out of the water and stood on the wonderfully warm smooth rock, facing the sparkle of the sun on the fjord. Now she played, one by one, the seven songs which she had chosen for the second movement. Because her violin represented the choir, she played each song four times: as *soprano*, as *alto*, as *tenor*, and as *bass*, keeping clear in her mind how each voice sounded with the other three.

After finishing the seven, she went back to the first song and went through it again, playing the cello part. Reaching down into her violin's deepest notes, (though still an octave or two above an actual cello), she played, through seven songs, the unrelentingly rolling *basso continuo*.

Her violin rendered every voice in the choir, as well as the cello, through verse after verse of all seven songs. Later, she would add a Russian song, and a Sami *yoik*. But for now, she had rendered seven of her grandfather's favorite songs into something symphonic.

People walking along the sidewalk behind her, people coming out of the museums, people putting ketchup on their hot dogs, all stopped to listen to the young woman who sometimes stood in the water and sometimes stood on a dry rock, while on her violin she played a multitude of variations of songs which most of the people recognized. The gathering crowd did not applaud, for the musician rarely stopped playing, and anyway, she faced the fjord. She certainly was not playing for money, for her violin case lay closed on the grass. She seemed to be composing, or arranging, or orchestrating, and she did so with great passion, sweeping her bow back and forth with absolute concentration.

And then, after a long moment of silence, while a hundred people listened to the lapping applause of the sea, the woman began to play again. Her audience heard something different. She was not playing songs anymore, but something extended and majestic and hauntingly melodic.

The musician was clearly oblivious of the crowd gathering along the grassy shore behind her, while she played as if the fjord were her audience. And now—she peered up—a pair of passing gulls became part of her audience, for she carved a quick *cadenza* and sent it up to them. Then she seemed to be playing for the sun, for she lifted her face to the yellow-white disk and played a sort of march. Her music grew with a slow *crescendo*, as if her violin's voice were reaching to the far end of the fjord, where the fjord opened into the sea.

And then she seemed to be playing for a distant red sail, a tiny crimson spinnaker near Nesoddtangen, on a tiny sloop plying north up the fjord. The woman—standing now up to her knees in the cold water—played a fanfare, as if her violin were a trumpet. She played as if she were announcing someone's long awaited arrival.

Eli Margrethe skipped right over the last two sections of the second movement: the storm that struck the fleet, and the dirge that followed. She would write the dirge this summer, while she stood in the seaport cemetery.

Instead, she moved right into the unwritten third movement, and now composed it. She played a love song: a love song for the sea and the islands and the mountains that she had missed for six long years. She rendered her homesickness into love, rendered her love into music. She rendered her longing into celebration. She quickly discovered a new melody, a melody that lifted on the wings of a sea eagle, the big-shouldered bird that rode the wind blowing off the sea and sweeping up the side of a steep mountain. Her music sailed, her music soared, as she looked down at her northern world through the eyes of an eagle.

Without even trying, she would remember the best of it; she understood the structure of the movement even as it developed; she anticipated each key change. She could write it all down later, home in her box.

After she had played in this manner for perhaps forty-five minutes—the red spinnaker had grown incrementally larger—she knew that within all she had played, she could use at least half of it. She had composed, in one sweep while standing beside the sea on a Saturday afternoon, a complete rough draft of her third movement.

Lowering the violin from her shoulder, she yelped a loud cheer of triumph out to the fjord.

When clearly the woman had stopped playing, the crowd on the strip of grass behind her broke into a roar of applause. Utterly surprised, the woman turned around and stared at her audience.

The people of Oslo were applauding her third movement! Holding her violin and bow well above the water, she bowed gratefully, left, right, and center, to her exuberant listeners.

"Bravo!" called someone, perhaps a tourist from Italy.

For the first time, after six long years in the city of Oslo, Eli Margrethe began to feel at home.

CHAPTER 20

Lillian and Bjørn had arranged with Harriet, Lillian's grandmother, that they would meet at the Sognsvann trolley stop at noon
for a picnic. Harriet would ride the trolley down from Holmenkollen to the station at Majorstuen, then change for the trolley north to
Sognsvann, as she had done hundreds of times before. She would
carry (as she insisted) a small picnic basket. (Bjørn had brought ad-
ditional provisions in his backpack.) Lillian and Bjørn would walk
with Harriet from the Sognsvann platform to the lake, then they
would follow the path along the shore to a picnic table in a grove of
white birches.

During lunch today, Lillian would ask her grandmother the
question which she had waited for years to ask. For she might be a
mother now. So it was finally time to learn about her own mother.

Harriet, who had turned eighty-five last September, had suggested the picnic, so they could celebrate. Lillian had spoken with
her grandmother several times about her decision to have a child.
Harriet said, "Ja, I would like to hear that voice before I go." Harriet knew to the day when Lillian had stopped taking the pill, and
she had no doubt that this camping trip would prove to be a grand
success. She would have joined them beside the lake for a picnic
even if she had to bring an umbrella; but today, the blue sky and
bright sun would bless her every step.

When the three red cars of the little train pulled up to the
Sognsvann platform, Lillian saw Harriet's face smiling out from the
front window of the first car.

The train stopped, its red doors slid open, and a crowd of hikers
and families and a half-dozen bikers poured out. When Lillian and
Bjørn stepped into the nearly empty car, they saw Harriet making

125

her way along the aisle. She was gripping a seat back with one hand and holding a large picnic basket with the other.

Bjørn took the basket, accepted a kiss on the cheek, then he offered his arm to Harriet: an arm as solid as a railing, a railing which would follow her wherever she wanted to go. Bjørn led Harriet out the door of the trolley into the sunshine, then they walked side by side, gentleman and lady, her hand on his arm, along the concrete platform toward the earthen path to the lake.

Lillian walked behind them, watching them with a smile. Bjørn wore a sleeveless blue T-shirt, with thin blue straps over his gorgeous shoulders. He was dark and lean and as graceful as an otter, and full of fun like an otter. He was joking now with Harriet, telling her about the smoke in his eyes this morning while he was trying to make coffee on the campfire.

As she watched them walking ahead of her—Bjørn and Harriet, grace and graciousness—Lillian rejoiced in her family. Never mind her father. Stiff as a tombstone. She had her family of three, and soon, she hoped, four.

The three picnickers walked past the big parking lot, followed the paved lane, passed through the gate, then stepped onto the soft black earthen path, full of fresh footprints and old pine cones. They followed the path to the southern tip of the lake: a tiny bay, frozen now, where in the summer infants could bathe in the warm shallow water. The path forked to make a loop around the lake; they took the right fork and followed the path along the lake's eastern shore. They shared the path with hikers and joggers and chattering children, all of them finally liberated from the cage of winter.

Harriet paused, as she always did, to admire the Three Sisters: three gracefully curving birches that stood together on the rocky shore of the lake, one of them with a heart carved into its white bark. In the summer, the white trunks were lovely against the blue of the water; they were still lovely today against the gray of the ice.

Harriet wore her old brown hiking shirt and trousers, and her summer hiking boots, as if she were setting off from the lodge at Finse for a long day's hike across the high mountain plateau of the Hardanger. Without her grandmother and those mountains, Lillian doubted that she would ever have learned to play the flute, or have survived her high school solo performance, or have made it through the College of Music. Harriet and the Hardanger had enabled her to achieve such a level of artistry that her audition at the Symphony had been successful.

And certainly, without Harriet and those wild rocky ranges, there would be no Bjørn.

Harriet nodded with approval as they approached the sunlit picnic table in a grove of birches; the twigs of the birches were faintly swollen with red buds. The table was about ten meters from the edge of the frozen lake. Relinquishing Bjørn's arm, Harriet sat on the bench looking out toward the lake. Bjørn set the picnic basket on the table, then sat on the bench beside Harriet. Lillian walked around the table and sat across from her grandmother, facing the forest. She was almost ready to ask about her mother.

Reaching with hands that had built a hundred campfires above the timberline, Harriet opened the big wicker basket and served an undisputed triumph of a summertime picnic lunch. She had bought two loaves of bread at the neighborhood shop; the loaves had baked early that morning. She lifted jars and tubes and cans out of the basket: every possible type of herring and goat cheese and berry preserve that a person might want to put on her bread.

Bjørn unzipped his backpack (which he had left on the table when he and Lillian walked down from the pier to the trolley station) and took out Lillian's contribution. Inside a plastic food box, well tied with a string, was her first potato salad of the season. Inside a second box was her lemon cake.

Harriet now lifted out of her wicker basket—Lillian marveled at the weight which her grandmother had carried—a stainless steel thermos. Bjørn took three battered aluminum cups from his backpack and set them in a row on a gray weather-beaten board of the table. With her old fingers gripping as strongly as they could, Harriet unscrewed the steel cup on the thermos and set it aside. Then she poured her coffee into the three camping cups; the arc of coffee caught the sunshine and shone deep amber as it filled the cups.

Lillian smelled the coffee. She knew it had been brewed from beans ground at the grocer's this morning. Not like her father's powdered cardboard coffee. Her grandmother's coffee was a skier's mountain coffee, tasting of long white slopes and majestic white peaks.

Only after Lillian had tasted the coffee—she blinked her eyes with surprise——did she realize that her grandmother had added to the coffee a goodly portion of rum.

Lillian giggled at Bjørn, "Try your coffee."

Bjørn wrapped his strong conga-drummer's fingers around the old battered cup, lifted it to his lips and took a sip. Then he grinned. "Harriet!" he exclaimed with a laugh. Bjørn's laughter boomed out over the lake; Lillian heard its faint echo.

After lunch, and a second though smaller cup of coffee, Lillian looked across the cluttered table at her grandmother and asked her, "Will you tell me about my mother? About who she really was."

Lillian did not want her father's version anymore. She wanted the truth.

"Ja," said Harriet, handing her plate to Bjørn, who set all three plates on the far end of the table. "You are ready now. You have your Bjørn. Together, you are strong enough."

Before, they were still "the honeymooners." Now, they were possible parents. Harriet folded her hands on the table. "Your mother, Katerine Vidgis Thorp, was born in the mountain village of Voss in 1950. Her parents knit sweaters in a factory. And, though I hate to bring him into the story, your father, my son, was born in Oslo in 1950. His parents had launched a small shipping company, which proved to be very successful.

"Katerine and Morten grew up in their separate worlds, then they met at the Business College in Bergen. Both of them were very bright, you see. And motivated. Morten studied economics so he could take over the family business one day. Katerine studied economics so she could learn why the poor countries of the world stayed poor. This was in the late Sixties, early Seventies, and your mother was very swept up by the new ideas of brotherhood and peace. She might have become some sort of a hippie, but she was always a quiet girl from the quiet village of Voss. She didn't need the beads. She read book after book in the college library, often exceeded the reading list for the course.

"She should have gone on to the University of Oslo. She should have gotten a master's degree in third-world development, and maybe even a doctorate. But instead, she listened to Morten. Who professed that he loved her. They graduated together in May of 1972, they got married in July. Boom boom.

"You, Lillian, were born ten months later. Your two brothers followed, one every second year, as planned. Thus, Katerine was married in Seventy-two. First child in Seventy-three. Second child in Seventy-five. Third child in Seventy-seven."

Harriet lifted her folded hands an inch or two above the table, then set them down again. "Now a number of other things happened during this time. Six months after you were born, your mother joined Save the Children. She began to attend a monthly meeting in a home near the University of Oslo. Your father would not let her travel to any conferences outside of Oslo, so she could never advance up the ladder with Save the Children. She would have made a wonderful group secretary, and no doubt, with her economic background, would eventually have been offered a job at the main office. But people at such a level of responsibility must of course be able to travel throughout Norway to meet with other branches of Save the Children. And anyone working in the main office would certainly have to attend conferences throughout Europe.

"But Morten would have none of that. 'Your job is here with your children,' he told her. No wife of his would be staying at some foreign hotel.

"So, while continuing as a neighborhood member of Save the Children, your mother joined Amnesty International. She joined about three months after Svenn was born. While you and your brother took naps, she was writing letters to governments and prisoners around the world. Morten consented to buy her a desk, so she could turn a spare bedroom into her office.

"Then, during the summer of 1977, when you were four years old, your mother did the oddest thing. Or at least, it seemed odd to me. And Morten was utterly baffled.

"Katerine read an article in the newspaper about a Norwegian nurse who had been working in a hospital on Sri Lanka—the island I had known as Ceylon. The nurse was killed there when someone opened fire on the ambulance she was riding in. She, her patient, and the driver were all killed. Her body was flown home to Oslo. The newspaper said that a funeral with honors would be held at Vestre Aker Cemetery.

"Your mother, pregnant with your second brother, arranged for a baby-sitter to watch you and Svenn. Then she went to the funeral. It was a warm but rainy day in July. Most of the people in the cemetery had umbrellas. Your mother did not. She stood off by herself in the rain and wept as if that nurse had been her sister.

"When the service was over, and people were leaving, Katerine walked forward and stood alone beside the fresh grave. The nurse's brother (as he explained in the police report) noticed that a strange woman was standing alone in the drizzle beside the mound of wet earth. He thought that perhaps she was from some mental hospital. Perhaps she had somehow managed to escape. He decided that he should notify the police.

"The police brought her home. She was soaking wet, and absolutely silent. Everything that Morten and I learned, we learned from the police and from the baby-sitter. Katerine never said a word about attending the funeral. Three months later, she gave birth to a healthy baby boy.

"So in January, February, and the first half of March, 1978, she was the wife of Morten the Executive, and mother of three beautiful children. She had a fine home in the Holmenkollen section of Oslo, and a train ticket whenever she wanted it to Voss, so the children could visit their grandparents. And I was living in the house next door, the original house on the land, wondering if, when, and how much, I should step into my son's family.

"Then in late March of 1978, Norwegian peacekeepers went into Lebanon. Norway joined about a dozen other countries in sending trained professionals—over seven hundred infantry, and over two hundred in logistic units—in a United Nations effort to curtail the violence in southern Lebanon." Harriet lifted her folded hands, set them down again. "Your mother could have explained much more than I can about the details of that war. She read every book she could find on Lebanon and Palestine and Israel. She followed the news in the papers and on television about border skirmishes and shelling.

"In June, three weeks after the peacekeepers had arrived in Lebanon, your mother announced at the dinner table—dinner was usually a silent affair during which Morten mulled over the problems of the day while Katerine fed the children—that she wanted to become a nurse. She told Morten about the Norwegian medical team in Lebanon. One day, she wanted to join them. Most of the nurses and doctors had families in Norway, she had learned. They served for a limited time, then they returned to their families and their jobs. Katerine wanted to wear, she told Morten, the United

Nations blue beret.

"Morten stared at her as if she were some utter stranger. He said quietly, 'No, you are not going to become a nurse.' He refused to discuss the issue any further. Katerine became silent. For one week. Then she hired a baby-sitter to watch her three children every afternoon and evening, seven days a week, and began working as a cook at the Oslo Salvation Army, down at Majorstuen in the heart of the city. She worked with the other kitchen volunteers, peeling potatoes, slicing cheese, and mixing dough for fresh bread. She was gifted at it. Within a month she was preparing over a hundred dinners a day. Her recipes were her mother's recipes, from Voss.

"She was profoundly happy during those six months. During half a year. She enjoyed every morning with her children, and every afternoon and evening with her other family, her big and jovial and compassionate family. You were five then, so you may remember those mornings."

"Yes," said Lillian. "She would take us on hikes in the forest. When the snow came, we skied. It was summer and fall, and a part of winter. For only a few hours every morning, and then she would disappear."

"Ja. Be kind to her, Lillian. For half a year, she was happy. Until just before Christmas, when Morten the Executive needed his wife at the company Christmas banquet. He needed her in a formal dress, perhaps with a festive sprig of red holly on her lapel, seated beside him at the head of the table.

"Katerine told him, 'No.' She would be working in the Salvation Army kitchen that evening.

"So Morten drove down to the Salvation Army at Majorstuen on the evening *before* the banquet, walked through the dining room without introducing himself to anyone, and found your mother in the kitchen, where she wore a simple blue dress and a blue kerchief over her hair. She and the other volunteers were singing some old song together while she sweated over a pot of potatoes and a pot of codfish.

"Morten ordered her home. She shook her head and said, 'No.' He tried to grab her arm, but she dodged him and then she slapped him across the face. Slapped him in front of half a dozen other volunteers. Outraged, and no doubt already thinking about a divorce, Morten stormed out of the kitchen. He drove home to plan his

Christmas banquet, and his excuse for her absence."

Harriet stared at Lillian for a long silent moment. "Katerine did not go home after work that evening. The police report states that she may have been sighted on Kirke Street. If so, she was crying while she was walking in a heavy snowfall.

"Then she vanished." Harriet lifted her hands, set them down.

"The police did not begin their search until noon the following day, for Morten was not so quick to phone them. It was an embarrassment, you know.

"Boys with sleds found her, at about two in the afternoon. They had been walking through the Vestle Aker Cemetery when they discovered a dead woman in a blue dress, covered with a few centimeters of snow, lying beside a grave. Not on a grave, but *beside* one.

"The police, whom the boys notified, noted that the person in the nearby grave was a nurse who had died in 1977 while serving in Sri Lanka. Your mother lay down next to that Norwegian nurse, and died.

"She had taken off her coat and thrown it a short distance away. It too was covered with snow. Then, in the thin cotton dress which she had been wearing in the hot kitchen, she lay down beside her sister."

Harriet thumped her hands on the table. "That was your mother."

Then she shook her head with a weary sigh. "Your father of course wanted you to know nothing about all that. His version to his five-year-old daughter was that Mommy had been hit by a car while crossing a street in a blizzard."

Harriet narrowed her eyes with anger as she spoke the long-hidden truth. "But it wasn't a car. It was your father, my son, who slowly murdered your mother. Suffocated her for six and a half years."

Harriet unfolded her hands, then startled Lillian by slapping one hand on the table. "So when Morten threatened to prevent you from going to the College of Music, I stepped in." She leaned forward toward Lillian with a wry smile. "Do you want to know the truth? I threatened to fire him. Fire Mama's boy. Because I own the company, you see. He works for me."

She sat up straight with a smile of profound satisfaction. "So now, my Lillian, you have your symphonic flute, and your very own timpanist. Soon, you will have a little vocalist whose first *aria* will be a healthy wail."

Leaning forward, she reached for Lillian's hand, then for Bjørn's hand. "I thank you, my dears, for this great joy in my life."

"You are most welcome," said Bjørn.

But Lillian was quiet. She could see her mother so clearly in that Salvation Army kitchen.

"And now, Lillian," Harriet squeezed Lillian's hand, "maybe you might play a little something for your mother. Letting her know the good news."

"Ja," said Lillian. "Ja."

Lillian reached into her backpack, pulled out a long thin black leather case. She opened the case and fitted the two pieces of her flute together.

Then she walked with her flute to the shore of the lake, where she stepped out on a smooth rounded limb of rock, a small peninsula of glacier-polished granite, part of the bedrock of Norway.

She did not look down at the gray ice of the lake, nor across at the green-black fringe of the forest, but up and up and up at the celestial blue sky. Turning briefly to the south, she raised her silver flute, which had once been Harriet's silver flute, with a gesture of gratitude toward the sun. Then, turning north, she lifted her face toward the blue sky and began to play.

She sent up long silver ribbons of music, long silver ribbons rippling with a bit of *vibrato*. She sent her silver ribbons up to the blue sky, each ribbon laden with love, and joy, and profound happiness that at last they had found each other.

She was no longer an orphan, and her mother was no longer without a child.

Part IV

Tuckets and Flourishes

CHAPTER 21

Inger the Indomitable, together with Johannes the Thunderer and Voldemar the Sharp-Eyed, sailed their sturdy craft, the *Strongheart*, up the last stretch of the rolling blue fjord toward the ancient seaport of Oslo, capital of the Kingdom of Norway. The three sailors stared at the twin square towers of City Hall, a brick bastion overlooking the northernmost tip of the fjord. They could not see the Concert House, hidden behind a jumble of buildings to the left of City Hall. But soon they would walk upon the ancient timbers of the wharf, and upon the ancient stones of the streets, until they reached the Great Hall, where they would take their places as conductor, guest pianist, and concertmaster. They would be joined this evening by an orchestra of one hundred and seven fervent musicians. They would be joined as well by the people of Oslo in the audience, by the people of Norway listening to their radios, and by the people of Estonia, receiving the concert via satellite.

Inger, steady at the wheel with her crew flanking her, said to Voldemar, "First mate Keskküla, would you take the wheel, please? I want to make a pot of galley coffee."

She could tell that Voldemar was enormously pleased to be invited to take the wheel. He stood in readiness beside her, then wrapped his hands around the spokes as she let go. (Johannes stepped forward into the cockpit, so not to be in the way.) Inger and Voldemar peered together at the old brass compass: the sloop held a course of 45 degrees. Then they scanned the water ahead: a cluster of large islands to starboard, the Dyna lighthouse to port. A large black-and-white ferry, *Dronningen*, was approaching in the distance on its trip from Oslo to Nesoddtangen, but Inger's course kept the sloop well west of the ferry route.

They ran their eyes over the white mainsail, the white jib, the red spinnaker: all three were in excellent trim.

"All right?" she asked, looking at Voldemar.

"All right," he said, watching the telltales.

Stepping forward into the cockpit, Inger motioned to Johannes that he could take his place again beside the wheel. He nodded, then stood beside Voldemar at the helm.

Inger looked at her two men, shoulder to shoulder, Voldemar in his blue shirt and jeans, Johannes in his brown shirt and slacks, master and apprentice, peering together now at the compass. Leaving the ship in their capable hands, she went below to make a pot of sailor's coffee.

Johannes could hear, coming up the hatch, Inger's voice. She was singing down in the boat's little kitchen, singing the song that she had been humming in the car this morning on the way to the farm. Her voice was very quiet, as if she were singing to herself. He could not always catch the words, but he recognized the song as Sissel's "The Seed."

Inger's voice lifted with the second verse, becoming a bit more confident.

She sang the third verse loudly enough that he could hear, "When a night has frozen hands that want to grip your soul, . . ."

He wondered what nights she had been through. No one could have lifted him out of his coffin except someone who had once been in one herself.

Now she sang, her lovely voice soaring,

"Take your wisdom from a winter,
That has covered all life with snow:
Deep in the earth's labyrinths
Grows the shoot from a seed."

Then she was quiet; that was the end of the song. She rattled a pot on the stove. Ja, thought Johannes, that woman is an entire garden, waiting to sprout, waiting to blossom.

Voldemar could smell the coffee vapors coming up the hatch. "You know," he said to Johannes, "Beethoven used to make his own coffee. He always made good strong coffee for his guests."

"Hmm," said Johannes.

"Do you know what else he made strong?" asked Voldemar.

"Strong?"

"Yes, strong."

"You don't mean more developed, more powerful, more complex."

"No, *strong*."

"I give up. What?"

His eyes sweeping back and forth across the fjord, watching for other vessels, islands, buoys, Voldemar said, "The piano."

"Hmm."

"Beethoven learned to play on a five-octave spinet, a delicate instrument built for the lively, delicate music of Haydn and Mozart. But Beethoven as a young man in Vienna played a different sort of music. His powerful fingers often hit the keys so hard that inside the piano, the hammers broke the strings. Beethoven demanded a stronger piano, and spent his life in a running conversation with piano makers in Austria, France, Germany, and England. Finally, toward the end of his life, the Broadwood Company in London sent him, as a gift, a piano with six octaves, and a heavy frame of wood inside. The frame was strong enough to support the enormous tension in the strings. Broadwood provided almost every note with four heavy strings rather than three, with the hope that the deaf composer might be able to hear them.

"Shortly after Beethoven's death, pianos were made with an iron frame. The steel frame in the Steinway waiting for me now in the Concert House is the final evolution of Beethoven's demand for a piano strong enough for the hands that played his music."

"Ja," said Johannes, "so Beethoven was responsible for strong coffee and strong pianos."

"Exactly. And something more. His belief was very strong. Which was important, because he believed in *us*. He lived in the age of Napoleon, an age of kings and tyrants and a tzar, and of unrelenting war. He earned his money from the fickle aristocracy. His publishers were, some of them, outright thieves. And yet he wrote music about Brotherhood, and Joy, and a God in Heaven. He wrote music for the ages, and he sent out his encouragement to every age. Because he believed in us."

"You are right," said Johannes. "He believed in us. Or he never would have given us the concerto that you will play tonight."

"Exactly. And what I want you to know—"

Inger called up through the hatch, "Could you speak a little more loudly, please? I can just barely hear you."

"Of course," Voldemar called down. With a bit more volume, he continued, "What I want you to know, about the concert tonight, is that Estonia, like Beethoven's piano, is slowly growing very strong. And I want, tonight, Johannes, to play with hands that are very strong." His hands steady on the wheel, he stared at Johannes. "An orchestra is not strong, it is powerful. I am asking for a very powerful orchestra."

Johannes nodded that he understood. "As powerful," he said, "as Beethoven's dream of Brotherhood. As powerful as Estonia's dream of Freedom. Will that be powerful enough?"

"Yes. That is exactly powerful enough."

Inger came up the steps with a blue restaurant mug in each hand, steaming with coffee. She held the hot mugs with old faded pot holders, so that she could offer them handle-first to her men. She gave one mug to Voldemar. "You will hear the Tchaikovsky. You will hear the Rossini. When you sit down on your bench for the Beethoven, you will know what sort of orchestra you have."

Voldemar let go of the wheel with one hand to take the mug. "Thank you. Yes, I will be listening."

Inger gave the other mug to Johannes. He took it with a handsome smile, and a glint of something in his eyes.

Then the two gentlemen waited while Inger went back down the steps to fetch her own mug of coffee. When she returned to the deck, she stood to the right of Voldemar, and thus welcomed him to continue at the wheel.

Then, together, the three of them in a row, their feet spread against the gentle rocking of the sloop, drank the sort of strong coffee that rightfully follows a superb dinner of codfish.

CHAPTER 22

Astrid, accompanied by her family of fifteen, including three daughters and their husbands and children, and accompanied as well by her seven students, along with their parents, grandparents, and siblings, waited on the sunlit platform of the Lillehammer train station for the 15:16 train to Oslo. At 15:10 by the clock on the brick station, she walked to the edge of the platform and looked north at the empty rails. Then she turned and looked south at the sun gleaming on the rails: the two long silver stripes reached toward her destiny tonight. She wondered how Inger was doing with Johannes. Without a concert, it was going to be a long and dismal train ride home tonight.

Magnus, holding her cello in its black case, was talking with Trond, her eight-year-old student, who had already spent two years waiting for his little hands to catch up with his prodigious talent. Magnus and Trond stood apart from the large cluster of her entourage, talking, no doubt, about their mutual passion for fishing in the high mountain lakes. Spring was here; the ice would soon be gone. The trout were waiting.

Magnus glanced across the crowded platform at her, gave her a nod, then went back to talking with the boy. Magnus could talk with children forever. He always wanted to know what they liked to do, where their strongest talent lay. For he too was a teacher, preparing his students for something far more than a job.

Magnus had spent fifty years on the mountain, teaching skiers how to read the slopes, how to cut an edge, how to tuck, how to balance speed with safety. He had coached countless teams by the time he retired at sixty-eight, after fifty winters of showing kids how to race down the mountain.

He had started coaching when he was eighteen, able to outski anyone on any mountain in all of Oppland County. He never really wanted to win a race. After he had won them all, he discovered that what he really wanted to do was coach other kids to win the race. That's what he loved to do. So he did it, for half a century. Because Magnus, a child of war, as Astrid was a child of war, believed that if Norway had enough skiers, she could never be permanently conquered.

Magnus trained military skiers as well. He was occasionally gone from Lillehammer for months at a time, training troops on the Finnmark tundra. He taught the young men and women, dressed in white, how to vanish on the snowy tundra, how to ski great distances as ghosts, how to carry out whatever task they were assigned; then how to vanish again.

He loved the north of Norway, far above the polar circle. One night, on a solo trek, he skied a loop of fifty-two kilometers (as he judged on his map), at 22 degrees below zero, when the perfect dry snow was lit by the green and pink glow of the northern lights.

Magnus believed that if Norway could field, at any time, any moment, ten thousand men and women who could vanish on skis into the mountains, then Norway was safe. For most of those ten thousand would never be caught.

Her beloved Magnus. He always told her that she was his favorite student, although she did not venture now beyond the lower hills. She loved to watch him ski down the slope ahead of her: he sailed over the snow with long graceful curves, as if he wore angel's wings.

She remembered when they were young: she had always been with him at the top of the mountain before a race. Standing to one side and a bit below him, in the cluster of coaches, she watched his face during the last few seconds before he started out the gate. His winter-blue eyes stared down the steep course like the eyes of an eagle about to descend from the heavens.

"Train three twenty-four to Oslo," called the station's loudspeaker, "now approaching on track one."

Magnus glanced at her again and waved that he was coming. People on the platform looked north at the approaching train, picked up bags, called for children. Those who were staying kissed those who were leaving. Two or three who were late came running from a nearby parking lot.

The long red train swept into the station, slowed, and came to a stop. The pneumatic doors slid open. Magnus now stood beside her with her cello. For a moment, while she admired the handsome red train, lit by the bright afternoon sun, a train that she had loved already as a girl of five, Astrid said a brief prayer of gratitude to whatever Spirit it was that had given her these seventy years.

Then, joining the flow of students and daughters and grandchildren—and Magnus carefully carrying her cello—she boarded the train for the two-and-a-half-hour journey to the station in Oslo, where her entourage would nearly double.

CHAPTER 23

Per Olaf stood in front of the tall oval mirror in his bedroom—
a mirror which had reflected his father, his grandfather, and three
patriarch farmers before them—tying the black tie which he would
wear at the symphony tonight. Ingeborg sat in front of her own mirror, fastening a brooch. Neither spoke, for what more could they
say about the question which had loomed with a heavy presence all
through the day: would there, or would there not, be a concert tonight?

He pulled the knot tight, straightened the black tie down the
front of his white shirt. His thoughts, ever moving back and forth
between today's impending disaster and tomorrow's fervent dream,
remained optimistic. He believed in Inger, in Johannes, in Voldemar, in professionals working together in a good and honest world.
And he wanted to believe that they were working together toward
something more than just a concert tonight.

He put on his black coat, straightened the shoulders, tugged on
the cuffs.

For several years now, Per Olaf had wanted to do a certain thing
in Ås.

But he wasn't sure whether or not he should. It wasn't the sort
of thing one did in a quiet Norwegian town.

Today a train would pull into the station at Ås at 16:35, a train
which would take him and Ingeborg and Anne Cecilie and Odd to
the station at the National Theater at 17:07. Then a ten-minute walk
would bring them to the Concert House, or to the harbor. Nor-
mally, they would meet a variable group of members of the orchestra for dinner at Vegeta Vertshus, a restaurant on Munkedam's
Street on the way to the Concert House. Dinner at six, at the Hall
by seven, and the concert at eight. But that was back when the clock
in heaven was ticking right.

This afternoon, the four of them would walk straight to the harbor, to see if a sloop (a boat with one mast and two white sails, as Inger had explained to him on the phone), with a dark wooden hull, not a white fiberglass hull, was sailing toward the wharf. "If you see a tall red sail pulling the sloop," she had told him, "then you'll know that Johannes is ready to conduct the concert. If no red sail, notify Arne."

So the question was, When did a person give voice to his optimism, to his faith? Would he just hold his breath and hope until he saw that red sail, or would he reach beyond today to the dream of tomorrow, and announce that a better world was on its way?

Ja, the question was, How to greet the train at Ås?

All passengers heading north from Ås to Oslo had to be on the eastern platform. Driving from the farm and through the village of Ås, Odd would park on the western side of the tracks. Then the four of them would walk, he with his trumpet, Anne Cecilie with her oboe, up the steps and across a pedestrian bridge over the tracks, then down the steps to the platform for the northbound train.

For several years now, he had wanted to announce the arrival of the Saturday 16:35 with the trumpet solo in Rossini's "William Tell." He wanted to stand up on the pedestrian bridge over the tracks, like a troubadour on the turret of a castle; when the train from Moss first appeared, he would play his jubilant fanfare for the people waiting on the platform. To let them know that the train today was no ordinary train, for it would take them to some extraordinary destiny.

If, they were willing to make the journey.

He wanted to announce that train, to the kids at least. The older folks were usually preoccupied with their stock market closings and car repairs and the latest world disaster. But the kids, they deserved a fair chance in the world. They should be able to Build, not just Clean Up. We do not pass on to the next generation merely our poor petty riches, but the world itself. The kids needed to hear something other than modern noise. Maybe the call of a trumpet could awaken a bit of hope, a bit of confidence, in a bored child waiting on the platform on a Saturday afternoon with his mother and father for the train to Oslo. Maybe that trumpet, calling down from the blue sky, could announce to every kid that he, that she, was fully able to become a galloping hero.

The kids could begin living tomorrow's dream, today.

Then why hesitate any further? Play your fanfare for the kids, then hurry down the steps so you don't miss the train.

Per Olaf pulled open the top drawer of his dresser, reached among his socks and took out a brown aluminum tube about half a meter long, with a metal plug at one end, and a wooden cork at the other. To give what was inside the tube to Johannes would be an act of faith.

Tonight was the night.

CHAPTER 24

Eli Margrethe ate two hot dogs with ketchup, and a chocolate ice cream cone for dessert. Then she lay down on the grass in the sunshine, with her violin in its case beside her, and fell sound asleep.

When she awoke and saw how much the sun had swung to the west, she jumped up and hurried with her violin toward the pier behind the Fram Museum, to catch the next ferry to Oslo. Halfway to the pier, she asked an elderly gentleman for the time; she was enormously relieved that she was not late. The ferry would arrive in ten minutes; she would be at the restaurant by six o'clock, at the Concert House by seven.

But what if she had slept another hour?

Once she was on board the ferry from Bygdøy to Oslo, she realized that she was starving. The dinner at Vegeta—she always sat next to Astrid—was the one social event in her life. Both the dinner and the abundance of jovial company: she greatly looked forward to both.

Standing at the railing of the ferry's upper deck, she spotted, while looking south, Inger's red spinnaker. Inger, who had discovered Eli Margrethe in the student orchestra, and who knew of her homesickness for the sea up north, had invited her last September to go sailing. Several violinists from the orchestra were on board; it was a wonderful way to get to know them. With a good wind from the north, they had sailed south with the red spinnaker all the way to Moss.

After rehearsal on Friday, Inger had quietly announced to the orchestra that she, as concertmaster, would try to do something with Johannes on Saturday. Eli Margrethe wondered if Johannes was aboard the sloop. And what about the pianist from Estonia?

Oh, how that boy had suffered through the week. She was grateful to be a mere violinist in the second section, as quiet and unnoticed as a small gray mouse.

Her thoughts returned to dinner with Astrid. They would sit in one of the old wooden booths in the basement of the restaurant, in a room big enough for whoever from the orchestra showed up. And though Astrid always brought some of her students, she and Astrid would be able, quietly, secretly, while seated next to each other in the midst of conversation and laughter, to agree when they could get together, just the two of them, at Astrid's home in Lillehammer, so that Eli Margrethe could play for Astrid the cello part, on her violin, of the symphony in progress. First Eli Margrethe would play the part, then they would play it together, on violin and cello, until Astrid had learned it, and had added some innovations of her own. (They had done so with the first movement, before Eli Margrethe wrote the cello part into the score.) Once Astrid was able to play her part alone, Eli Margrethe could play the choir, through song after song . . . in a second movement that was becoming as vocal as Beethoven's fourth movement of the Ninth.

Perhaps she needed to expand her choir, beyond a chorus of thirty villagers. Ja, let the choir become something symphonic.

As Eli Margrethe's ferry approached a pier at the wharf in front of City Hall, she could hear in her mind a four-hundred-voice choir singing in the upper registers a song not from the sea, not from the mountains, but from the realm of the green and pink northern lights, pulsing and rippling over mountain and sea both.

Lillian and Bjørn ended their camping trip with a hot shower at Harriet's house. They dressed for the concert in the bedroom which had once been little Morten's, and which Harriet now called "The Honeymoon Suite." Bjørn kept his black suit in a closet there, and Lillian her three black dresses. Thus they were able to accompany Harriet to every concert.

At five o'clock, the three of them had a glass of red wine in Harriet's living room (where the big window faced away from Morten's house). They toasted to Inger's success. Then they walked down the street to the Hollmenkollen trolley stop. By six o'clock, they would be at the restaurant, where hopefully someone had some news about Johannes.

Lillian carried her flute in its slender black case. She would play tonight a song of welcome for Harriet's great grandchild. And she would play as well a song of welcome for her mother, who had never attended a single concert, not even a little girl's first performance.

While the three of them stood on the small neighborhood platform, waiting for the red train to come winding down around the curve, Lillian stood on Bjørn's left and held his strong, beautiful hand. Harriet stood on his right, holding his arm. Harriet did not want to sit down on the bench. Time enough to sit when the trolley came.

Bjørn stood on the platform in his black suit with black silk lapels, with granddaughter and grandmother flanking him. Both of them could be quick with a smile in their blue eyes, but both had a granite jaw of stubbornness. He loved them profoundly, these two strong women. Lillian was strong by virtue of her determination, and Harriet was strong by virtue of her bedrock sense of right and wrong. Together, they kept Morten in his place.

On a Saturday evening, the first warm sunny evening of April, Morten the Rigid was no doubt at home in his office, seated in front of his computer, clicking through his accounts to see if any payments were overdue.

At 16:34, the crowd on the northbound platform at the train station at Ås was jolted from its newspapers and cell phones and cigarettes and dull stares and last kisses by a thunderbolt from the blue. Swinging their faces toward the pedestrian bridge, they saw a man in a black suit playing a trumpet: he was announcing the train, which they could see now coming down the tracks, with the trumpeter's galloping solo in the "William Tell Overture."

One commuter wondered to his colleague whether this was the railroad's latest sales gimmick.

A dozen children looked up at the man with a trumpet and wondered, Was something special happening? Was it a special train today?

As the first red car rumbled beneath the bridge, the man knelt down and put his trumpet into its case. Then he hurried to the end of the bridge and scampered down the steps.

By the time the train came to a stop and its doors popped open, he was ready to board.

Anne Cecilie and Odd and Ingeborg and Per Olaf, grinning, stepped onto the train.

CHAPTER 25

With Akershus, the ancient stone fortress on a bluff overlooking
Oslo Harbor, at three o'clock off her starboard beam, the modern
buildings along Aker Wharf at eleven o'clock to port, and the twin
brick towers of City Hall, like the pins of an enormous cleat where
one could snub one's lines and moor one's soul, about half a kilometer beyond the bow, Inger was about to ask Voldemar and Johannes to douse the spinnaker, when she wondered if Per Olaf had
seen it. Had he notified the others in the orchestra that the concert
was on? Well, whether he had or hadn't, she needed to bring the red
spinnaker down, then get the motor running, and ready the rubber
bumpers over the side for docking.

"Strike the spinnaker!" she called to her crew alert on the bow.
Johannes released the halyard; Voldemar gathered armloads of red
sail as the limp and luffing spinnaker came slowly down.

She looked at her watch: five fifty-two. They would be
docked—if she could find a spot in the marina, or along the
wharf—by a quarter after six. Dressed and ready to disembark by a
quarter to seven. They would promenade along the wharf, walk to
the corner of City Hall, then stride up the long gentle hill on Haakon VII's Street, and arrive at the Concert House by seven. Johannes would have an hour to do whatever he needed to do with the
orchestra.

At eight o'clock, when usually her work was just beginning, she
could finally relax.

She readied the throttle, ran the blower, then started the engine.
She heard it rumble beneath her feet: with a bit of throttling, the
motor ran smoothly. She let it idle in neutral while the sloop now
sailed on its mainsail and jib. Voldemar stuffed the red spinnaker
back into its huge sail bag.

She ran the motor until it was warm, then shut it off. She would sail with her expert crew to within a hundred meters of Aker Wharf, then turn the motor back on and drop sails. With the motor, she would look for a spot among the piers in the marina.

Per Olaf, Ingeborg, Anne Cecilie, and Odd came up the subway escalator to the courtyard behind the National Theater. They walked at a steady pace down Olav V's Street toward the harbor. They were about to enter the park beside City Hall when Odd, who could spot a hawk circling half a kilometer away, pointed toward the fjord and shouted, "There's your red sail!"

Per Olaf stared out at the water, until Ja! He saw it, Inger's signal. Raising in triumph the hand that held the brown tube, he cheered, "Hurrah!"

They walked quickly through the park, then crossed the paved ferry wharf at an angle to the right toward the wooden wharf along the western shore, all the while keeping an eye on the red sail, which was becoming more and more distinct.

Per Olaf—hurrying ahead of the others now—walked past the restaurant boats moored along Aker Wharf. A group of people around an outdoor table held up a dozen glasses of golden beer in the sunshine. He heard snatches of a toast, then a burst of laughter.

He passed children playing on a replica of an old ship. He passed a woman playing Grieg's "Kind Greetings, Fair Ladies" on her accordion. He glanced back to see if the others were keeping up; they were about thirty meters behind. Then, searching the far end of the wharf, where a long pier lined with sailboats and motorboats jutted into the harbor, he spotted a vacant space near the outer end of the pier.

Breaking into a run, with his trumpet case in one hand and the brown tube gripped in the other, Per Olaf sprinted the last fifty meters along the wooden wharf, slowed a bit to manage the sharp turn to the left, then ran, with wings on his feet, past a two-masted yacht with *Aberdeen* scrolled in gold letters across her black stern.

Out in the harbor, Inger's red sail was coming down. But he had seen it, he had seen it. He would meet the sloop, get final orders, then race to the restaurant. The gang was waiting to hear about Johannes.

He slowed to a confident walk as he laid claim to the outermost twenty meters of the pier. Puffing, he set down his trumpet case on the weather-worn boards. Then he faced the sloop with its two white sails and waved his arms. But Inger was still too far away to see him.

He looked to the left across the harbor at the big clock on City Hall's eastern tower: five minutes to six. Inger was right on time.

Kneeling on the dock, he set the brown tube, not quite as long as his arm, on a gray plank, then he opened the trumpet case and took out his trumpet. He put the tube inside the case, closed the lid and snapped the latches shut.

He stood with his trumpet and watched the sloop, its smaller triangular sail coming down now as the vessel circled into the—Per Olaf wet his finger and held it up—south by southwest wind.

Holding his trumpet with one hand, he waved with big sweeps of his free arm. When Inger spotted him and waved back, he took hold of the trumpet with both hands, raised it to his lips and sent out over the blue water the bold brassy notes of his fanfare for Olav the Good.

Inger motored through a slow half-circle until she brought her bow into the wind; the flapping sails, like two tired white horses, puffed while they caught their breath. Voldemar and Johannes dropped the jib, and bagged it. They dropped the mainsail; Voldemar lashed it neatly along its boom.

Once the flapping sails were silent, Inger could hear, over the rumble of the motor, the faint but brassy sound of a trumpet playing a lively fanfare. She looked toward the pier where Per Olaf had been waving. She saw him holding a golden spark in his hands: his trumpet, gleaming in the sun. He had found a spot where she could dock. And now he announced, for all of Oslo to hear, the *Strongheart's* triumphant arrival.

For an old hermit farmer., he had done extremely well this past week.

As Inger brought the *Kristine Marie* slowly broadside to the pier, Voldemar tossed the coiled bow line to Per Olaf, who stood ready to catch it. Johannes tossed a coiled line from the stern to Odd. The sloop's rubber bumpers nudged the pier. Inger idled the motor in neutral, then turned it off. Tonight after the concert, when Martin brought her his bouquet of red roses backstage, she would thank him a hundred times for his ever reliable engine.

Once the lines had been cleated, Johannes in the cockpit called to Per Olaf on the pier at the bow, "We thank you for your tuckets and flourishes."

"You are most welcome," called back Per Olaf. He walked along the pier to the stern, then he reached over the railing and offered a brown metal tube to Johannes.

"Maestro," said Per Olaf, "I bought this in a shop on Nevsky Prospect in Saint Petersburg. Or, shall I say, we bought it. Because it is from the entire orchestra. We thought you should have it, from Russia, the next time you conduct Tchaikovsky."

Johannes looked into Per Olaf's steady blue eyes, then he bowed slightly as he reached over the railing and accepted the gift. He pulled out the wooden cork, lifted the other end of the tube: into the fingers of his right hand slid the wooden bulb of a white baton. The baton was just the right length, just the right weight, with a bulb of maple.

He raised the baton, a white stick in the blue sky, as if he stood on his podium, ready to signal the first beat. The new baton would replace whatever baton he had been using during rehearsals.

"Per Olaf," Johannes took the baton into his left hand, then he reached across the railing with his right hand so he could shake Per Olaf's hand, "you and the members of our great orchestra have my fullest apology. You have my profound gratitude. And you have a conductor for your concert tonight."

"Very good, sir. We have made arrangements that everyone will meet in the Hall at seven o'clock, so that we might take a quick look at the scores."

"Yes. Perfect. We shall have a brief rehearsal at seven."

Per Olaf looked across the harbor at the clock on City Hall: six-twenty.

"Maestro, will you join us for dinner at the restaurant?" Johannes had been absent from the orchestra's informal dinners for the past several months.

"Thank you," said Johannes, "but we have had Inger's codfish for lunch." He beamed a smile at her. Then he said to Ingeborg and Anne Cecilie on the pier, "And we have *devoured* your picnics as an early dinner."

"Yes," added Voldemar from the bow, "superb chicken. Superb

potato salad."

"You are welcome, you are welcome," replied Anne Cecilie and Ingeborg, greatly pleased.

Per Olaf picked up his trumpet case from the dock. "I'll let the orchestra know. Rehearsal at seven."

Then the four from the farm departed, leaving the three from the sea to get ready for the concert.

"All right, lads," said Inger to her men, "you have ten minutes below to put on your suits while I tidy up the deck. Then it's my turn." She pointed across the harbor at the clock on City Hall. "At six forty-five, we step ashore."

The golden-orange sun, low in the southwest, shone upon the brick ramparts of City Hall: the bastion defending all that is best in the human spirit glowed a golden red.

Voldemar and Johannes, in blue and in brown, went down the steps to their quarters below to change into black tails, white ties.

Inger walked forward along the dockside gunnel to the bow, where she inspected the lines. Then the whispered, "Thank you, Mama. Thank you, Papa."

CHAPTER 26

The train from Lillehammer arrived at the Oslo Station at 17:34. Astrid and her entourage disembarked; Magnus stepped carefully from the car to the platform with her cello. They could have ridden one more stop to the National Theater, arriving at 17:39. But Astrid wanted to walk from the Oslo train station along Karl Johan Boulevard, past the Cathedral, past the Parliament, past the Grand Hotel, past the park in the heart of the city, past the book shop, past the University, past the National Theater, to Munkedam's Street. The walk from the station to the restaurant took no more than half an hour; they would be at Vegeta by a quarter after six.

Her half-hour walk had a purpose. When the Lillehammer entourage entered the Oslo train station, they would be met by her other group of students. (Once a week, she rode the early morning train down to Oslo to give cello lessons to twelve refugee children, each one gifted and full of promise.)

About a month before her seventieth birthday, Astrid had agreed with all nineteen of her students that she would give them each a ticket to the concert tonight. She would provide tickets as well for their families, though she needed an exact count. (The ticket office had agreed to give her a rebate on the price. She had also made an arrangement with Vegeta Vertshus: since she was bringing a party of roughly sixty, the restaurant would lower the price of each dinner by twenty percent.)

Her Lillehammer students had already met most of her Oslo students, for Astrid had invited her Oslo students up to Lillehammer for several Saturday practice sessions in the auditorium at the high school. But none of the Lillehammer parents had yet met the parents from Oslo. Astrid thought that after the two groups had met inside the train station, the half-hour walk would enable them to get to know each other.

Thus when she led her entourage up the long walkway and into the enormous hall of the station, she was met by twelve families from seven different countries (or would-be countries), all of them, children and parents and a few grandparents, brightening into a smile when she appeared.

She spent the next several minutes introducing everyone from Lillehammer to everyone from Oslo, while people in both groups nodded greetings to each other. Then three people whom she had not yet met, a grandmother from the Kurdish mountains of northern Iraq, an uncle from Bethlehem in Palestine, and a young woman from Bosnia who looked at Astrid with shy and frightened eyes, were introduced to the two groups by their families. The woman from Bosnia had arrived in Norway only three days ago.

Astrid now had the great pleasure of distributing her birthday tickets. She had mixed them all up, so that when everyone found his or her seat, they would discover whom they were sitting next to. (She had bought five extra tickets, not knowing how many family members might decide, at the last minute, to come.) As she passed out the tickets, she heard the Norwegian word for Thank You, "Takk," spoken with a broad range of accents.

Then, with her Grande Entourage assembled and ticketed, she led the parade through the station, out the glass door, down the stone steps, and, carefully, across Fred Olsen's Street, to the eastern end of Karl Johan Boulevard, the main thoroughfare through the heart of Oslo. At the other end of Karl Johan—they would be able to see it well from the Parliament—stood the Royal Palace on a hill.

She listened to the chatter behind her as she led the long thin parade along a pedestrian street lined with shops. Glancing back now and then, she saw that the students were mixing well. The Lillehammer parents were doing an excellent job of talking, in Norwegian or in their best English, with the Oslo parents, who struggled with Norwegian, or used their best English.

Toward the front of the parade, Magnus was walking beside the young woman from Bosnia. He was telling her, in very slow clear English, about a Bosnian Olympic skier whom he knew by name. The woman smiled with recognition; she knew of him too.

Astrid pointed out the Cathedral to the right, then the Parliament to the left. Both buildings engendered renewed conversation in the group behind her.

The sun, low in the southwest, shone on their faces when they walked beyond the Parliament. The sun shone as well on a tangerine wrap-around dress from Pakistan, a dark suit with broad lapels from Iraq, a lime-green dress from Lillehammer. The trees in the park in front of the Parliament reached their bare branches into the warm sunshine. Astrid looked up at the pale silvery-blue sky of early evening, still without a cloud.

Traffic was light on the boulevard, but many people were out strolling on the wide sidewalks. Astrid led her parade past the Grand Hotel, past the ice cream shop, past the book shop, past the law department of the University. Then she paused at the corner, so that everyone could look up the last stretch of Karl Johan at the stately yellow palace, home of the royal family. The Norwegians in the group pointed at the balcony with tall white pillars, and explained to the people from other lands that on the Seventeenth of May, the King and Queen and their family stood on the balcony and waved to the children in their parade. Then Bayan, an eight-year-old cello student from Palestine, announced to the group in a proud voice that he had been in the parade last May, with his school, and had himself seen the Queen and King.

Astrid led the group—now not a long thin parade but an oblong cluster—across Karl Johan Boulevard, then through the courtyard behind the National Theater, to Munkedam's Street. As they walked along the sidewalk toward the restaurant, she looked at her watch: a minute short of six-fifteen. She had to be at the Concert House by seven, and so had half an hour for dinner. But her students and their families could stay at the restaurant until seven-thirty. Magnus would come with her. The short walk would give them a few minutes together, and a kiss before she went backstage.

When Astrid was about twenty meters from the Vegeta sign, with her Grande Entourage chattering and laughing behind her, Eli Margrethe stepped out the restaurant's door and looked up the sidewalk. When she saw Astrid, her face brightened and she waved. Astrid could tell with one look that Eli Margrethe had been working on her symphony, and that she had made progress. She recognized Eli's shy confidence.

"The second movement?" called Astrid.

"Ja, the vocal section," called back Eli Margrethe as she hurried up the sidewalk. "And the third movement! All of it, right through."

"Congratulations!" Astrid reached toward Eli Margrethe and the two professionals shook hands. (She could not give her Composer a hug in front of such a group tonight.)

Eli Margrethe joined the Grande Entourage. She shortened her name to Eli as she introduced herself again and again.

Inside the restaurant, she went through the buffet line beside the young woman from Bosnia.

CHAPTER 27

Gathered at one of the old wooden tables in the restaurant's big basement were eight members of the orchestra, wondering together what sort of concert it would be tonight. At the end of rehearsal on Friday, Inger had told Jon Christian, who played bassoon, that she would try to get Johannes to phone Voldemar on Saturday morning, so they could arrange some sort of rehearsal. But no one had heard from Inger since.

Per Olaf had phoned Frode, who played trombone, at ten-thirty this morning, to tell him that Inger and Johannes had just been at the farm, and that the plan was that Inger would sail with Johannes and Voldemar on her boat from Drøbak to Oslo.

Per Olaf told Frode about the red sail, and that he would be on the wharf watching for it. He would bring the news, good or bad, to everyone gathered at the restaurant.

But it was now six-fifteen, and still no Per Olaf.

Haavard, who played French horn, had just been talking on the restaurant telephone with Bente at the symphony office, and with Edvard in the sound studio. Neither one of them had heard from Inger either. Edvard was going to demand, at the next board meeting, that every damn member of the orchestra carry a cell phone at all times.

Giuseppe, the lone Italian in the orchestra, who played the clarinet, shrugged his shoulders with a grin and said, "You Norwegians, so temperamental!"

Ingmari, who played viola, said to Ulf, who played bass, "Wouldn't it be something if we had the old Johannes again? Remember his 'Messiah,' that Christmas concert about four years ago? The entire audience stood up at the end and roared with applause."

"Hmm," said Ulf. "He's got it in him, somewhere buried beneath all that rubbish."

In the adjoining booth, Bjørn sat next to Harriet; Lillian sat across the table from them. They shared the booth with several of Astrid's students, one of whom, a boy from Kashmir, identified the strange vegetables mixed in with the restaurant's rice. Lillian was watching Magnus come down the stairs with two cups of coffee, no doubt one for himself and one for Astrid, when suddenly Per Olaf appeared grinning on the staircase behind him, with his trumpet.

Looking down over the railing at the booths and tables, Per Olaf played the first triumphant bars of his Rossini solo, *allegro vivace*. Everyone understood immediately: Johannes, somehow, somewhere, was ready. A thunderous cheer filled the room.

Per Olaf announced, "Inger, who has performed a miracle today, will be walking with Johannes and Voldemar up Haakon VII's Street in about half an hour. Johannes would like to meet for a brief rehearsal at seven. I suggest that we finish our dinners and be on our way along Munkedam's Street by six forty-five. At the corner, at about six-fifty, we might be able to greet our Maestro."

"Hurrah!" shouted Frode. "An excellent plan!"

Per Olaf, Ingeborg, Anne Cecilie, and Odd managed to have a quick dinner, while they told everyone about the sloop's red sail, and how well Johannes had looked when the sailboat docked at the wharf.

At six forty-five, the Grande Entourage, consisting now of members of the orchestra, students of music, family and friends, rumbled up the stairs from the basement to the main floor of the restaurant, nodded to the staff that dinner had been excellent, then poured out the door. Everyone turned to the right and followed the Munkedam sidewalk toward the corner.

The sun, hidden behind the buildings on the right, shone with an orange tinge on the shop windows and stone facades across the street.

Per Olaf, already at the corner, stood on the opposite side of the street beneath a hairdresser's sign. He was peering around the edge of the building toward the lower part of Haakon VII's Street.

CHAPTER 28

At the top of Haakon VII's Street, just below a statue of Haakon VII himself, a television crew from the Norwegian Broadcasting Company was interviewing people on camera as they strolled to and from the cafés on Ruseløkk Street on this first warm Saturday evening in Norway. "And how did you spend your day?" asked the jovial announcer as he extended his microphone to people with pink cheeks and sunburned noses.

Part way through someone's shy giggle and mumbled reply— definitely a bit of tape which they would *not* use on the news tonight—the announcer heard, from somewhere down Haakon VII's Street, a trumpet playing a fanfare. It was a spirited fanfare, magnificent and bold. Looking down the street, he saw three people in black walking up the broad sidewalk: a woman between two men. He spotted the trumpeter on the corner across the street, playing with the bell of his trumpet pointed toward the three in black. Now he recognized Johannes Berg, Maestro Berg, probably on his way to a concert which he would conduct this evening. And the woman was Inger Magnussen, principle violinist. The second man . . . the announcer, who covered a broad array of news events, did not recognize him.

But something was up. For now a crowd was pouring out of Munkedam's Street and gathering in a sort of jubilant parade behind Maestro Berg. The parade proceeded up one sidewalk while the lone trumpeter walked up the other, playing fanfare after fanfare, as if to announce . . . to announce what?

"Get the camera on them!" called the announcer to his cameraman. "Get the street, get the crowd, then zoom in on the three in black. Get the trumpeter. Hurry that sound boom down there! Now pan back to the three in black. Zoom in on Maestro Berg, on the left. Now on Inger Magnussen, in the middle. Now on the fellow on the right. Lars, run down and find out who that second fellow is."

The announcer was ready, as the three in black reached the top of Haakon VII's Street, to ask them if they would say a few words into his microphone.

Maestro Berg said, "No time. We've got a rehearsal at seven." Then he turned to the left and led the parade of roughly a hundred people—various individuals carried a French horn case, a flute case, a bassoon case—along Ruseløkk Street toward the sculptures at the entrance to the Concert House.

Part V

Allegro Appassionata

CHAPTER 29

Johannes went to his office in the Concert House, saw the cot with a rumpled sleeping bag on it and cringed at what he had been. He picked up his Tchaikovsky score, his Rossini score, and his Beethoven score, held them all in one hand while he held his baton in its brown tube in his other hand. Then he left the ruins and wreckage behind him as he closed his office door. He walked with butterflies in his stomach toward the entrance to the stage.

As he stepped through the door between the dim backstage waiting room and the brightly lit floorboards of the orchestral stage, he saw with a glance that the members of the orchestra were in their seats with music and instruments ready. The last bit of conversation quickly quieted. Now, accented by the perfect acoustics of the Concert House, there was only the sound of his footsteps walking across the front of the stage to the podium.

He laid the Tchaikovsky score on the angled wooden lectern of the podium, then set the other two scores on a shelf below. He set his baton in its tube on the lectern. He opened the Tchaikovsky to the first page, ran his eye down the first measure, and felt the old reassurance as he read the music: while most of the orchestra remained silent, the cello and contrabass began their sustained groan. After three beats, the bassoon came in, a soul awakening in a grave. Scanning the next few measures, he could hear the music deepening, growing slowly more powerful.

Ja, he could do this.

He glanced down to his left at Inger, watching him with a look of professional confidence. He realized that for the first time in his life, he was going to conduct a symphony concert for a woman whom he loved.

He looked at Astrid, seated almost directly in front of him, and saw not the slightest hint of censure or blame. He had almost ruined her last season with the orchestra, for in June she would retire. Her eyes were sparkling with eagerness as she waited for the Maestro to begin.

"Good evening," he said to his one hundred and eight professionals. "I want to tell you," he looked from face to face, in the string sections, in the woodwinds, in the brass, "that I am profoundly sorry for what I have put you through. From deep in my heart, you have my fullest apology."

A few of the musicians nodded. Most kept looking at him, waiting for more.

"I would also like to say, Thank you. Thank you for being here tonight. I am deeply grateful."

Again a few nods. Otherwise, one hundred and eight faces, each beautiful in its own way, continued to watch him.

"Ja. I believe our brief rehearsal tonight should focus on *tempi*. I think if we start each movement of the Tchaikovsky, then of the Rossini, and then the Beethoven, we'll be together on each tempo change."

He paused, then he added, to reassure his orchestra, "I can tell you that our guest from Estonia, and I, have had a very successful rehearsal of the Beethoven Concerto."

"*Very* successful," echoed Voldemar, sitting in the third row of the empty theater. Johannes looked behind him to his right at the young man who had brought more hope into his life than he had felt for decades.

Turning again to his orchestra, he held up the brown tube for all to see. "Per Olaf," he nodded with a smile of gratitude to Per Olaf in the trumpet section, "has told me that this Russian baton is a gift from the orchestra. I am honored. Profoundly honored."

He pulled out the wooden cork, tilted the tube and caught in his fingers the maple bulb. He put the cork back in place and set down the tube on his tilted lectern. Then he raised the long, nearly weightless white baton in readiness.

Bows were readied; a foot shuffled; then silence.

Johannes conducted the preparation beat: Astrid and her cellos, Ulf and his contrabass section, and now Jon Christian on his bassoon, came in perfectly.

Rehearsal ended at seven twenty-five. As the musicians vacated the stage, the theater doors were finally opened. The crowd which had been impatiently waiting in the lobbies now poured into the theater and dispersed to seats *parterre* and in the balcony.

Backstage, Voldemar climbed broad white marble steps two at a time up the staircase to the fifth floor, where the Norwegian Broadcasting Company had its radio studio. Edvard, seated at his control panel with headphones on, gave him a thumbs-up. "We're linked. We're ready. Two minutes ago, I spoke with Anu. She asked me to tell you that she loves you."

"She said that?" He felt her presence, the protective strength that she wrapped around him, his armor, as he forged his way forward.

"Ja. She said they've been announcing you all week. Every radio in Estonia is tuned in tonight."

"Good. Thanks."

He went back down to the third floor, circled behind the dimly lit stage to his Steinway (waiting in the left wing), reached out his hand and gave the piano's closed black lid a confident pat. Then he stepped quickly down the stairs at the left edge of the stage, walked up a side aisle of the theater—weaving against the tide of people coming down the aisle—and climbed a theater staircase to the balcony. He walked up the steep aisle to the last row of seats, about two-thirds filled. He sat in a vacant seat at the left end of the middle section, ready to relinquish the seat if someone with a ticket claimed it. (But no one did.) He listened to the excited hum of the audience around him as he stared down at the dim orchestral stage where, in about an hour and a half, Beethoven's strong hands would address the world.

Following the brief rehearsal, members of the orchestra had half an hour to take a quick shower and change (if necessary) into their black suits and dresses; to find something to eat and a cup of coffee in the backstage cafeteria; and to savor the extraordinary energy in the Hall tonight. The Maestro had been his old self. Full of fire and confidence. Ready with a quick smile, ready with a tempo that promised they would all soon be playing some powerful music.

"We're recording, you know," the musicians told each other,

though everyone knew.

"Ja, tonight's the night."

CHAPTER 30

At five minutes to eight, the members of the orchestra assembled on the spotlit stage. As they sat on their chairs or stools, or stood behind their drums, they glanced out at the audience and saw that almost every seat in the Hall was filled.

Anne Cecilie raised the twin reeds of her oboe to her lips, sent her breath between the reeds and played a perfect A. She held the note while the concertmaster tuned her violin to that A. The strings now tuned, and then the rest of the orchestra joined in. Each instrument matched Anne Cecilie's A, then tuned up and down its own registers.

Anne Cecilie repeated her A, until she could hear that every string, every woodwind, every brass, was in tune.

Thus she brought order to her tiny universe, that it might flourish and prosper through Tchaikovsky's Sixth Symphony.

Inger, standing beside her chair at the front of the string sections, held Anne Cecilie's A on her violin. Listening carefully, she heard the other violins holding it too. She looked to the back row of the second section, for she always gave Eli Margrethe an encouraging smile. She stared with surprise: the usually pale and sad-looking girl was a healthy pink, and she was smiling with the first real happiness that Inger had ever seen in her face. Inger beamed back a smile, while she swept her bow and ran her fingers up and down the strings, listening carefully to each note.

When she sat in her chair, the violin ready in her lap, she looked down to the right at Martin, seated in the theater's first row. He and her parents had sat there for years; now he alone never missed a concert. He grinned as he pretended to hide with an arm the bouquet of red roses in his lap.

Then she looked up to the back of the murmurous Hall and saw

Voldemar in his black suit, seated at the left end of the last row in the balcony.

Per Olaf had alerted her that Voldemar was out in the audience.

After the rehearsal, Per Olaf had kept his eye on Voldemar, and thus had watched him descend the steps from the stage to the seats, then head up an aisle. Per Olaf followed at a discreet distance, for this behavior was highly unusual. The guest artist had his own private room beside the conductor's room, where he could wait without anyone disturbing him until it was time for him to perform. But Voldemar was not sitting in his room; he had visited the studio on the fifth floor, then had returned to the third, had entered the stage from the left wing and paused for a moment at his piano. And then he did what no visiting artist ever did: he joined the audience. For, as Per Olaf could see from the bottom corner of the balcony (where he was well hidden by the crowd taking their seats), Voldemar had found a seat at the very top of the balcony. Wearing his black suit (but without a suitcase for a last-minute dash to the airport), Voldemar paid no attention to the people milling around him, nor to the couple chatting beside him, as he stared down at the empty stage.

Per Olaf hurried to the backstage cafeteria, found Inger having a cup of coffee, and told her that Voldemar was seated in the balcony. "Should Johannes know?" he asked her.

Ordinarily, no one would see Johannes Berg until he came out of his room to conduct the opening piece. So the question was, Should they knock on his door?

Inger said, "Voldemar told Johannes on the boat today that he would be listening. And so he is. No need to disturb the Maestro."

Per Olaf nodded. "Ja. Good."

As she warmed up with a deep vibrato, Astrid looked down from her chair at Magnus, seated directly in front of her in the front row. Fifty-five years ago, he had sat in the front row of the school auditorium. His blue eyes had watched her so attentively then, and his blue eyes still watched her as attentively now.

Her mother would be listening this evening to the radio in her room. Every radio in the nursing home would be turned on. Well, they would hear the "William Tell" twice in one day!

Then Astrid thought, as she always did before a concert, about the woman to whom the cello really belonged. While she ran up and down an octave, she swept her gaze slowly across the front rows of the audience, searching for a woman her mother's age with a special look in her eyes.

This was Astrid's last season with the symphony. The rules had been stretched, but now at the age of seventy, she must retire. She would continue to play her cello as a member of a string quartet in Lillehammer. She would play *Birkebeiner* for another ten years, until young Trond, now eight years old, was eighteen. She could already hear what was inside him, waiting. Waiting for his hands to grow and strengthen. When Trond was eighteen, she would present him with *Birkebeiner*. Not as a gift, but on loan. She would tell him the cello's story. She would explain that no one could ever own *Birkebeiner*, they could only keep the cello for awhile, perhaps half a century or more, during which time the musician must enable the instrument to fulfill its promise: to help people over the mountain to safety, to freedom, to a new life.

Tonight, after sixty years, she still held the cello and its bow in her hands. As she continued warming up—running now up and down the highest notes—she scanned the audience, searching for the faces of her nineteen students, some from up on the mountain, some from the battlefields of war. She smiled when she spotted her two hooligans sitting together. Bayan, the eight-year-old boy from Palestine, wearing a blue coat, white shirt and red tie, sat beside Trond, wearing a black coat and white turtleneck. They had clearly swapped their tickets with someone so they could sit together.

She watched Bayan as he pointed to the towering pipes of the organ on the wall to the left of the stage. He made some comment to Trond. Trond nodded, then explained something to Bayan.

Bayan, a gifted cellist, was unable to listen to his own national orchestra because he had no nation.

Eli Margrethe knew that every radio would be on in Henningsvær. Her father, who had never spent a penny on any such fancy stuff, had bought the best radio and speaker system he could find in Svolvær, so the family could listen in the living room to her concerts. Neighbors of course came to visit on those evenings, with a loaf of hot bread and a folding chair. Her father always claimed that he could hear *her* amidst all the other violins.

Several of the fishermen in the village had installed better radios on their boats, so they could listen to her concerts while they were out at sea.

No one in Henningsvær ever called them "the Oslo Symphony concerts." They were always "Eli Margrethe's concerts."

Well, soon she would have her own concert. Her own symphony. Even if it took five years. It would be her gift to her people, back home.

While Lillian played up and down the registers of her flute, sending her silver notes to join the clamor around her, she looked out at Harriet, seated about half-way back in the *parterre* middle section, where Harriet considered the acoustics to be "perfect." Harriet would listen for the flute that had once been her own flute, and would enjoy, as she often told Lillian, "hearing what I had played well, played beautifully."

Tonight, Lillian would play her flute for a tiny creature now no more than a ball of cells. Welcome, welcome, a song of welcome. Welcome to a world where we grieve, and where we celebrate. A child within her, life within life.

And tonight, Katerine, wearing an elegant blue dress, sat in the audience with her fellow volunteers from the Salvation Army, as proud as a mother could be.

Lillian glanced over her shoulder at Bjørn, leaning down with his ear almost touching the skins of his timpani while gently he tapped them. She did not whisper to him, but merely stared for a long moment at the father of this new life.

Then she turned around in her chair and sat properly with her flute in her lap. Seated in the woodwind section, she was entirely surrounded by the orchestra, which was about to embark on Tchaikovsky, Rossini, and Beethoven. No ball of cells had ever been better lullabied than her child would be tonight.

Per Olaf blew out his spit valve one last time, then glanced up at the last row in the balcony, where once again he spotted Voldemar in his black suit. Did even a single person in the audience know that the featured artist tonight was sitting up there with them?

Bjørn knew that every radio in Televåg would be on tonight. His family and neighbors, out on their island of rock, snug in houses that could fend off any oceanic weather, would be listening for the sound of his timpani to emerge, as it occasionally did, from the sound of the rest of the orchestra. People in Televåg really liked it, they told him, when he thundered on his drums.

In his own home—a red house with white trim, perched on a granite ledge above the harbor, a new house built after the Germans had destroyed the entire village of Televåg during the war—his proud father kept two pictures on the pine wall over the radio in the living room. One was the old photograph of Bjørn playing his conga (with blurred hands), and the other was a professional photograph of the Oslo Symphony Orchestra.

Standing now behind the arc of his four brass kettledrums, their skins perfectly tuned, Bjørn listened as the last few musicians still tuning became quiet. Now the entire Hall was silent, waiting for the entrance of the Maestro.

He looked down at Lillian, seated in the heart of the orchestra. He could see her long blond hair, her pink cheek, the way she sat in the chair. And her hands restless on her flute.

During that long moment of silence (when every member of the orchestra should be as quiet and motionless as possible), Lillian slowly turned her head toward Bjørn and blew him a kiss.

Johannes, standing in the conductor's room, could feel the rolling motion of the sailboat. He was rising and falling, rising and falling on the gentle waves. The Tchaikovsky score was waiting for him on the lectern, opened to page one. His Russian baton lay atop the score.

He thought he ought to say something, by way of a brief prayer, before he opened the door and stepped out. He remembered his mother's words, could hear her voice saying them, "Look, Lord, at what we can do."

Then he opened the door, stepped out into the hallway, and closed the door behind him. He strode through the dim backstage waiting room, took a deep breath as he passed through the door to the brightly lit stage, heard growing applause from the audience, strode across the front of the stage to the circle of light beside his podium, and bowed to the left, to the right, to the center.

He stepped up on the podium and picked up his baton, then he looked down to his left at his concertmaster. With a faint smile, she was watching him; she nodded that the orchestra was ready.

He swept his eyes over the strings, the woodwinds, the brass, the percussion, saw that every section was ready.

He raised his baton.

CHAPTER 31

Now the beautiful transformation began for one hundred and nine people, as all ruminations vanished and the music became everything. They lived all week through the mundane drudgery for this moment when they broke free . . . and entered together a world completely different. All thinking was thinking within the music. They lived for this peace, this freedom, this challenge, this beauty.

As Johannes conducted with his new baton the *adagio* beats, the contrabasses began the piece, as the contrabasses would end the piece, with their faint deep murmur, the only sound within the vast silence of death. Now the bassoon crept up from the depths: a soul awakening in its grave. That soul had been given the ability to remember its life, one last time. It could revisit childhood, but only with a deep longing and melancholy sadness. It could recall a glimmer of joy, but only if shock and devastation could bring back their old pain. That strong and hungry and unrelentingly sensitive soul would be allowed to waltz in the second movement, and to march with triumph and jubilation in the third. But in the fourth movement, *adagio lamentoso*, with the contrabasses playing a heartbeat, the bassoon, creeping back down into the grave, relinquishes all memory of life. The heartbeat, *pianissimo*, diminishes to *pppp,* then stops. The cellos murmur for a moment, then they too are quiet within the vast silence of death.

A long moment . . . a very long moment . . . the longer the better . . . and then Johannes could hear the applause behind him. Emerging from the silence within himself, he swept his eyes with jubilation over the faces in his orchestra. His magnificent people had played the Tchaikovsky as well as he had ever heard them.

"Bravo!" called a voice from the balcony, a voice which Johannes recognized immediately as Voldemar's. Johannes turned around and bowed to the audience, left, right, and center. He held his hands up as if he would cup the last row in the balcony, then he opened his arms to embrace the entire audience.

He could hear the orchestra behind him tapping on their strings, on a timpani head: the applause he most loved. With a sweep of his arm, he beckoned the entire orchestra to stand and take a bow. The applause roared.

He glanced at Inger, beautiful and proud in her black dress. She had known from the first cup of coffee at dawn that together, they could do it.

He exited the stage, was called back twice for a bow. Each time, he swept his arm and bid the orchestra to stand. Bowing to them, he clapped his hands to the different sections with sturdy applause.

When he exited the stage a final time, he did not walk to his conductor's room, but to the little cafeteria, where the musicians could slice their own fresh bread and cover it with Anne Cecilie's homemade strawberry jam. They could fill a white china mug with strong coffee, and bask in the warm sunshine of friendship.

CHAPTER 32

Aboard a wooden sloop at anchor off the northern coast of Estonia, two couples sat in the cockpit and watched a huge orange sun setting over the Gulf of Finland; watched, looking beyond the stern, the sky to the north darken to a deep turquoise; watched the April stars appear in a sky of lucent black, while they listened to the four movements of Tchaikovsky's symphony on the sloop's radio.

Voldemar's father, who like the others was waiting for the third part of the program, squeezed his wife's hand as they sat beside each other on the wooden bench. He could see, lit by the pale glow of the stars, tears on her cheek. For while she listened, while the four of them listened, they were taken back to the past; they were made to think of the buried and unburied dead. It was good, of course, to remember the past, to keep that memory sacred. And of course tonight, when they would be enabled to think of the future, they had to pause first and remember the past bloody century, at least.

After the contrabass had plucked the final note, the two sets of parents, Voldemar's and Anu's, sat in utter silence. When the radio buzzed with applause, Anu's father reached his hand to a knob and turned off the volume. There would be an intermission now.

The four parents could hear gentle waves caressing the hull, as if it were a cradle at sea.

Murphy sat on the farmhouse porch, listening, his ears cocked, to the first frogs croaking and peeping in the night.

He stepped off the porch, trotted past the garden, then bounded along the ridge and down the hill; more dirt than dog, he was a rambling shadow beneath the stars.

When they heard him approaching, the frogs in the pond at the end of a gully became immediately silent. But after Murphy had sat quietly facing the pond for several minutes, one frog peeped, another croaked, and then the rest took courage and sang with unremitting jubilation.

During the intermission, Voldemar stood in line with everyone else, waiting to pee.

Eli Margrethe knew, as she sat in the crowded cafeteria with a cup of mint tea, that she had just played her best. She loved to be surrounded by so many friends. She made no effort to join their conversation. She wanted to savor, while Per Olaf told some joke, the glow of knowing she had just played her best.

Inger cut several slices from the brown block of goat cheese, laid them neatly on her three crackers, then stood to one side of the cafeteria and watched Johannes as he praised—one by one, scattered up and down the narrow room—the entire woodwind section. Lillian blushed. Everyone saw Lillian blush but no one said a word, because Johannes was speaking.

Standing beside the table where he had set his plate of bread and jam, he now addressed the French horn section; he did not simply praise them, but "marveled" at the tones they had achieved. Johannes looked each musician full in the face for a moment, as if he were discovering, and savoring, a long lost friend.

Continuing, as if at a banquet, at a feast, he turned to the contrabasses, to the percussion, to the cellos, the violas, and then to the violins. He was clearly delighted that a man could have so many good friends.

His blue eyes turned finally to the concertmaster. She was eating a cracker with goat cheese.

"I think," said Johannes with a proud smile, "that I should ask Inger to take a special bow. For without her, the orchestra would not have a conductor tonight."

She heard the immediate and hearty applause from the entire orchestra. Per Olaf called out, "Bravo!"

Perhaps blushing a little, she bowed to accept their gratitude.

CHAPTER 33

Astrid began Rossini's overture with a solo lamentation. A wail of grief. She always heard a woman crying, after the devastation of war. The other cellos came in, murmuring with compassion.

Grief has her say, and then comes the storm.

Peace follows with Lillian on her nightingale flute, Anne Cecilie on her soothing English horn. The world has time to breathe.

A triangle plays the sparkle of sunshine on rippling water.

And then . . .

Per Olaf delivered his galloping fanfare, announcing the arrival of the Hero. He could not lift the bell of his trumpet toward the last row in the balcony, but in his mind he sent up every bold and brassy note to the young man in a black suit, bidding him Welcome. And promising, on behalf of the entire Oslo Symphony, to be the orchestra that such a Hero would require.

When the trumpets came in, Voldemar felt a shiver go up his back. He sat up straight in his seat. This was clearly a powerful orchestra. This orchestra might well make itself heard in Estonia.

CHAPTER 34

Following the Rossini, the orchestra did not leave the stage, for it took the workmen no more than a few minutes to roll the black Steinway into position and lift its sounding board.

During those few minutes, every member of the orchestra—as well as the conductor himself, standing in the right wing—could see a lone figure in a black suit walking down the long steep aisle of the balcony. The figure descended a staircase, then walked down a side aisle on the ground floor. Voldemar hopped up the steps two at a time to the spotlit stage, then vanished into the left wing.

He stood alone backstage, with an eternity of time for a brief prayer. "Lord, behold your servant.

"I play tonight for the dead. For the dead of my country, and for the dead of my oppressor. Hear the voice of your servant, Lord, asking to be an instrument of your work. Tonight I play for the dead of every war since the beginning of human conflict. May all who died in war hear me in their graves around the world.

"I play for them with remembrance and compassion.

"And I play to reassure them that the human quest has not ended. Because while I play for the dead, I play as well for the children of Estonia, for the children of the world.

"May the children hear no more cannons, no more guns, no more bombs, no more land mines exploding beneath their bare feet. Rather, let the children hear the sound of wisdom, read aloud as poetry; the sound of wisdom, rendered by an orchestra into music; the sound of wisdom in an ocean wave, in the gurgling murmur of a springtime brook.

"Let us forge a new covenant, Lord, among the peoples of the world: to share the land, as the land would have us share it. Let us

185

bury no more anguished dead. Let us raise no more fettered children. Let us believe in this miracle of flesh and sense and love called man. Yea, let man forget his dominion, and find rather his purpose and place.

"I play tonight for tomorrow's child. I play with strength and care and love, as one day I, with strength and care and love, will build an oaken cradle."

He clenched his hands together. "Amen."

Then he walked along the dim hall backstage from the left wing to the entrance to the right wing, where he stood shoulder to shoulder beside his conductor. Out on the stage, the orchestra was tuned and quiet. The piano stood ready. The audience was silent, save for a few last coughs.

"Fine sailing with you today," said Johannes quietly with a warm smile.

"And fine sailing today with you."

"Although the conductor usually precedes the soloist to the stage, thus being in a position to welcome him, I suggest that you and I walk on together."

"As a team."

"Yes, as a team."

On the sloop anchored off the coast of Estonia, Voldemar's parents could hear on the radio the applause of the Norwegians: strong steady applause for the entrance of their son.

In her studio with her headphones on, Anu could hear Voldemar's footsteps as he walked across the stage to his piano. She heard him shift the bench slightly, heard him sit. She heard the conductor stepping up on the podium.

Then all was quiet.

CHAPTER 35

Inger formed a triangle with Johannes and Voldemar: the pianist was closer to the conductor than was the concertmaster, and closer as well to the front of the stage. With her violin and bow absolutely ready, she was able to watch the moment when Johannes, on the podium with the baton in his hand, looked down to his left at the pianist; Voldemar, looking past the Steinway's black sounding board at the conductor, nodded that he was ready.

Johannes turned to the orchestra and raised his arms, the white baton poised.

Voldemar poised his hands above the keyboard.

That first orchestral chord, E-flat major, filled the Concert House with an affirmation of strength; Bjørn struck the timpani firmly. The piano sprang out of that chord and filled the Concert House with an affirmation of extraordinary skill. Offering a promise of strength, a promise of joy, the orchestral chord and surging piano *cadenza* filled rooms in nursing homes, filled rooms in houses built on rolling farmland, on granite islands, on snow-clad tundra, filled taxis nudging forward in traffic on Karl Johan Boulevard, filled the cramped cabins of fishing boats, filled the open cockpit of a sloop, where Voldemar's father looked up at the stars that wrapped over the world as if they too were listening.

Astrid was celebrating her birthday now; her heart and the cello's heart were completely wedded now. *Birkebeiner* sang for the conductor who stood not on a podium but on a mountaintop. Her slender, powerful arm swept the bow back and forth as the cello section played no background *continuo*, but nearly as much melody as the treble sections. Most often, the orchestra spoke as one voice. Seated in the middle of the front row, wrapped by the vibrant arc of the orchestra from her left shoulder to her right shoulder, she could feel how much the musicians responded to the Maestro. This is what she wanted for her birthday: one magnificent concert in her last season, one evening with all one hundred and nine of them at their unrelenting best.

Eli Margrethe, who today had stood on her own mountaintop, now thought of nothing but the music she was playing. She heard the violins of section two, heard the violins of section one. She heard the piano, heard the brass. But above all, she followed the conductor, watching keenly for any change of tempo. The baton was not beating time, but signaling the heartbeat of the music. *Molto piu animato*, much more lively. *Tranquillo*, peacefully. *Leggieramente*, lightly, as soft as starlight.

As Voldemar completed the first movement at triple *forte* (with the entire orchestra backing him at double *forte*), Per Olaf thought, "Voldemar, you come as a fanfare, as the bold call of a trumpet, announcing to the world through tuckets and flourishes that the sun has risen upon Estonia."

In the long silence that followed, between the first and second movements, Voldemar's mother let out a breath of relief, of astonishment. "He did it," she said to her husband. "Our boy did it."

"That was just the first movement."

"I know. This is a little bit like the night he was born. The same magic. The same miracle."

"But not so rough on his mother this time."

She smiled. "No, not so rough on his mother this time. He's a big boy now."

"He's a young man," said Anu's father from the other side of the cockpit. "Young and strong."

From where they were anchored, they could see—beyond the bow, in the distance to the south—the spotlit towers of Tallinn: a medieval fortress turret, gothic and baroque spires, Russian Orthodox onion domes, and the skyscrapers of contemporary commerce. To the east, to the north off the stern, to the west: the dark sea wrapped around the land. Tallinn. Here was a port from which people sailed in every age with fervent hopes.

Now they heard the muted violins, and the contrabasses pluck-ing *pizzicato*, as the orchestra began the second movement, Beetho-ven's *Adagio*.

Johannes Berg did not lie in a patch of unmelted snow on the northern face of a mountain, but rather cradled an orchestra in his arms, glanced now and then at the intent face above the hidden hands running up and down the piano, and listened for shadings of change in Voldemar's tempo.

Their rehearsal aboard the *Kristine Marie* had served them well, for they moved now through the music in perfect tandem.

Lillian heard the music of heaven, where her mother lived. Up in that blue sky. And the man playing the piano: he was an angel as gentle as an angel could be, speaking quietly to someone who had once been deeply hurt, but who now might have recovered enough, might have regained enough of her old belief, that she could begin to think of singing again, singing with her friends in the kitchen.

But tonight, Mama, you are not in the kitchen, you are not working. You and your friends wear your silken dresses and sit in the best seats. You don't even have to sing tonight. I will sing for you. We will sing for you. Listen to me, Mama, when I play with the clarinet and bassoon. Listen to the oboe and bassoon together. Lis-ten to me, Mama, when we all play together.

Listen to me, Mama. Listen very carefully. You can hear a heart-beat within a heartbeat. Or at least, the promise of a heartbeat sometime in the next few months.

With that comforting thought, of a tiny fluttering heartbeat, Lillian turned her full attention to Voldemar Keskküla's exquisite trills.

When, at the end of the second movement, the bassoon and French horn carried the piano across the softest possible bridge to the third movement, Inger waited for her men to pounce on the *Rondo*.

* * *

Anu, at the control panel with her headphones on, listened as Voldemar finished sending his gentle benediction to his people, as if he plucked the notes from the stars and sprinkled them on those below.

When he launched into the *Rondo* of the third movement, she relaxed, let out a long breath, for if he got this far, he could sail through the rest. The third was always his favorite movement.

Voldemar knew that he was playing far beyond what he had ever played before. He also knew, in the back of his mind, that the concert tonight was being recorded. As he strode through the third movement—as confidently as Beethoven had once strode—he knew that he had fulfilled his promise. He had brought his gift to Oslo. And from Oslo, he would take a greater gift home.

As cadences flowed from his fingers, as he carved phrases of jubilation, as he marched in triumph, he let Beethoven prove anew that the human spirit was capable of touching the divine.

In the concluding bars, the orchestra became quiet while just the piano and the timpani played together. Bjørn played more and more softly, beneath the softening tones of the piano.

Then the piano took off alone on its final cadenza, a last grand flourish. The orchestra returned and marched to its final inexorable Beethovenian chord. A moment of silence, then the audience roared with applause.

Johannes stepped down from the podium and extended his hand to Voldemar, who stood up from the bench and shook the hand of the Maestro.

Both bowed to the audience. They saw that people were rising to their feet. Johannes gestured for the orchestra to stand. Beneath the thunder of applause, he told them, "Bravo! Bravo!"

He shook the hand of his concertmaster. He would have liked to kiss her.

She gripped his hand. "*Now* we have our Johannes Berg."

CHAPTER 36

In her small room with one window looking out on a dark courtyard, Eli Margrethe was writing in her notebook of manuscript paper. She had made a cup of tea for herself, but she had forgotten it and the tea had grown cold. She was working on the woodwind section in the third movement, especially the flute.

In Harriet's living room, with one candle lit, Bjørn and Harriet each had a glass of red wine, while Lillian had a glass of cranberry juice. They spoke quietly, as people do at the end of a day of celebration. Bjørn was talking about the beaches of Cuba, remembering how much he had liked running along the shore in the warm ankle-deep water. When he paused for a moment, Lillian announced that someday, when her growing family and her professional career would allow, she wanted to wear the United Nations blue beret.

"Ja," said Bjørn, raising his glass of wine, "we shall wear our blue berets together."

Astrid and Magnus sat in their bathrobes at the kitchen table, savoring a cup of hot cocoa. Their marathon day had ended; now they could sit in the quiet of the night.

"Do you know what I regret?" asked Magnus, looking across the table at Astrid.

"What?" she asked, puzzled by such a question.

"The eight years of your life before I met you. I regret that we didn't share those eight years too."

"Aren't sixty-two enough?"

"Jaah," he said like an old mountain farmer, and then he smiled at her, "and not a day lost in all those sixty-two."

In the farmhouse kitchen, Voldemar phoned Anu for the second time tonight (he had phoned her the first time right after the concert, from Edvard's phone in the radio studio on the fifth floor) while he sat at the table with Per Olaf and Ingeborg and Anne Cecilie and Odd, the five of them having a cold beer together.

The first phone call had been personal, between just the two of them. But the second call, to Anu now at home in her apartment in Tallinn, had a different purpose. Voldemar wanted Anu to say hello to his four Norwegian friends. They were having a little party and wished that she were there with them.

On the wooden sloop anchored off the coast of Estonia, Anu's parents slept on the bow, under the stars, while Voldemar's parents lay awake on the deck of the cockpit, under the stars. Snuggled in two sleeping bags which they had zipped together, atop an inflated camping pad, they were quiet, rolling gently with each wave that passed beneath the boat . . . until Voldemar's mother began to sing one of her grandmother's favorite songs.

Inger in her black dress, and Johannes in his black suit, walked together out the Concert House stage door to Haakon VII's Street, walked down the hill to the corner of City Hall—its red brick ramparts were spotlit against the night sky—crossed a bit of pavement, and then walked along the wooden wharf toward the *Kristine Marie*, where they thought they might have a nightcap of Grand Marnier.

They were strolling past one of the restaurant boats (still doing a good business at this late evening hour) when a musician playing background polka music on his accordion turned away from the noisy diners, faced the couple in black passing by on the wharf, and played, much more loudly than he had been playing before, a bit of Bach.

When Johannes and Inger looked over at him, he called, "Good evening, Maestro. Good evening, Concertmaster."

Inger and Johannes paused, pleased to have been recognized. People at the tables were turning toward them now.

The man with the accordion asked, "May I play a waltz for you?"

Johannes said, "Most assuredly."

While the bearded gentleman played the graceful waltz from Tchaikovsky's "Sleeping Beauty" ballet, Johannes took Inger's hand for the first time, then put his other hand around her back while she put her hand on his shoulder.

They began to waltz in long graceful circles across the wooden wharf. They whirled across lit boards in the light of electric lamps, they whirled across dark boards in the light of the stars. People walking along the wharf stepped aside, so that the strikingly handsome couple could waltz as freely as if the wharf had become their ballroom.

The author on Oslo Fjord

Photo by Lars Flæten

With a doctorate in literature from Stanford University in 1974, John Slade is a professor of English who has taught in northern Norway for ten years.

The author began this book on March 21, 2003, during the first hours of the War in Iraq. Devastated by the commencement of yet another war, he sat down at the typewriter to compose "the most beautiful and positive story that I could write."

Other books by John Slade

CHILDREN OF THE SUN

DANCING WITH SAMUEL

A JOURNEY OUT OF DARKNESS

HERBERT'S MOUNTAIN

THE NEW ST. PETERSBURG

ACID RAIN, ACID SNOW

COVENANT

A DREAM SEEDED IN THE EARTH

GOOD MORNING, DADDY!

BOOTMAKER TO THE NATION
The Story of the American Revolution

WOODGATE INTERNATIONAL
www.woodgateintl.com